CAMERON HAD BETRAYED SLOCUM DURING A TRAIN ROBBERY, AND SLOCUM WAS OUT TO GET HIM.

He changed his physical appearance and name so no one would recognize him. And he went so far as to make a deal with Cameron to steal more gold from the Dirty Dog mine.

Out on the prairie one night, as they were discussing their plans, Cameron drunkenly and proudly revealed a secret that bitterly hurt and angered Slocum—about a woman he had once loved.

Slocum knew the time had come to kill Cameron.

"Zesty and exciting, this brings a new and needed dimension to the classic Western."

WILLIAM DALE JENNINGS,
author of **THE COWBOYS**

OTHER BOOKS BY JAKE LOGAN

RIDE, SLOCUM, RIDE
HANGING JUSTICE
SLOCUM AND THE WIDOW KATE
ACROSS THE RIO GRANDE
THE COMANCHE'S WOMAN
SLOCUM'S GOLD
BLOODY TRAIL TO TEXAS
NORTH TO DAKOTA
SLOCUM'S WOMAN
WHITE HELL
RIDE FOR REVENGE
OUTLAW BLOOD
MONTANA SHOWDOWN
SEE TEXAS AND DIE
IRON MUSTANG
SHOTGUNS FROM HELL
SLOCUM'S BLOOD
SLOCUM'S FIRE
SLOCUM'S REVENGE
SLOCUM'S HELL
SLOCUM'S GRAVE
DEAD MAN'S HAND
FIGHTING VENGEANCE
SLOCUM'S SLAUGHTER
ROUGHRIDER
SLOCUM'S RAGE
HELLFIRE
SLOCUM'S CODE
SLOCUM'S FLAG
SLOCUM'S RAID
SLOCUM'S RUN
BLAZING GUNS
SLOCUM'S GAMBLE
SLOCUM'S DEBT
SLOCUM AND THE MAD MAJOR
THE NECKTIE PARTY
THE CANYON BUNCH
SWAMP FOXES
LAW COMES TO COLD RAIN
SLOCUM'S DRIVE
JACKSON HOLE TROUBLE
SILVER CITY SHOOTOUT
SLOCUM AND THE LAW
APACHE SUNRISE
SLOCUM'S JUSTICE
NEBRASKA BURNOUT
SLOCUM AND THE CATTLE QUEEN
SLOCUM'S WOMEN
SLOCUM'S COMMAND
SLOCUM GETS EVEN
SLOCUM AND THE LOST DUTCHMAN MINE
HIGH COUNTRY HOLDUP
GUNS OF SOUTH PASS
SLOCUM AND THE HATCHET MEN
BANDIT GOLD
SOUTH OF THE BORDER
DALLAS MADAM
TEXAS SHOWDOWN
SLOCUM IN DEADWOOD
SLOCUM'S WINNING HAND
SLOCUM AND THE GUN RUNNERS
SLOCUM'S PRIDE
SLOCUM'S CRIME
THE NEVADA SWINDLE
SLOCUM'S GOOD DEED
SLOCUM'S STAMPEDE
GUNPLAY AT HOBBS' HOLE
THE JOURNEY OF DEATH
SLOCUM AND THE AVENGING GUN
SLOCUM RIDES ALONE
THE SUNSHINE BASIN WAR
VIGILANTE JUSTICE
JAILBREAK MOON
SIX-GUN BRIDE
MESCALERO DAWN
DENVER GOLD
SLOCUM AND THE BOZEMAN TRAIL
SLOCUM AND THE HORSE THIEVES
SLOCUM AND THE NOOSE OF HELL
CHEYENNE BLOODBATH
SLOCUM AND THE SILVER RANCH FIGHT
THE BLACKMAIL EXPRESS
SLOCUM AND THE LONG WAGON TRAIN
SLOCUM AND THE DEADLY FEUD
RAWHIDE JUSTICE
SLOCUM AND THE INDIAN GHOST
SEVEN GRAVES TO LAREDO
SLOCUM AND THE ARIZONA COWBOYS
SIXGUN CEMETERY

JAKE LOGAN

ACROSS THE RIO GRANDE

BERKLEY BOOKS, NEW YORK

For the Big T

ACROSS THE RIO GRANDE

A Berkley Book / published by arrangement with
the author

PRINTING HISTORY
Playboy editon published 1975
Berkley edition / April 1987

For information address: The Berkley Publishing Group,
200 Madison Avenue, New York, New York 10016.

ISBN: 0-425-10025-1

A BERKLEY BOOK ® TM 757,375
Berkley Books are published by The Berkley Publishing Group,
200 Madison Avenue, New York, New York 10016.

PRINTED IN THE UNITED STATES OF AMERICA

10 9 8 7 6 5 4 3 2 1

1

A tall man with wide shoulders and a very dirty red sash lay flat on his stomach on the desert. He had taken off his old, worn sombrero and laid it on the hard-packed gray soil. His ear was pressed to an iron rail. From time to time he lifted his head and stared along the tracks stretching eastward to Socorro. His name was John Slocum, and he was going to rob the train. His heavy black mustache needed trimming.

After a few seconds he got up and walked 50 yards to the arroyo where his three men were waiting. His easy stride carried his 200 pounds lightly. The three watched his deliberate pace. No one spoke. The sun was almost straight overhead; it burned into the dry creek bed like a white-hot poker. Slocum took off his sombrero and waved it gently in an effort to make a breeze. His hair shone jet black, like an Indian's. His bandanna was soggy as he kept wiping his unshaven face.

Slocum shook his head. He did not believe in wasting words.

George Cameron grunted. "You're like a goddamn 'pache," he said. "Don' ever talk. Man oughta talk." He hitched up his trousers even though his new red suspenders were working fine. Cameron was new to the group. The man Slocum had been relying on had broken his leg in a stagecoach spill near Deming only three days ago. Cameron was available. Little was known about him. He had looked suitable to Slocum, who had vetoed Bond's objections. Now Slocum was beginning to feel that perhaps Bond was right.

Slocum lifted his head and stared at Cameron. His face was impassive but his ice-green eyes, now inflamed with alkali dust, seemed to Bond to drill through the sultry air like tiny acetylene torches.

After a few seconds Cameron dropped his eyes. Bond let out a long, relieved breath. Cameron undid the clove hitch he had made with his horse's reins around a dead cottonwood branch, moved it several inches along the branch and retied it. It was so obviously done to give his nervous hands something to do that Bond and the fourth man Dave Wells, began to titter.

Cameron spun towards Wells. Wells weighed only 150 pounds, 50 pounds lighter than Cameron. A mortar shell had fractured his left jawbone at Chickamauga and the regimental surgeon had been drunk. The right side of his face was permanently distorted. Cameron took a step towards the smaller man. With one fluid movement Wells pulled his carbine from its saddle scabbard and levered a shell into the chamber.

"Don' come any closer, you nutmeg-faced prune shitter," he said conversationally.

"Lousy li'l Johnny Reb!" Cameron hissed. But he had stopped moving.

"Enough," Slocum said quietly. Cameron and Wells stood glaring at each other.

"Enough," Slocum repeated. Very few of his friends knew that a faint scar ran across his scalp. He had been sabered at the Wilderness by a cavalryman, but he had managed to kill the man before he lost consciousness. Afterwards, he would experience savage, agonizing headaches. These frequently were the forerunners of sudden, violent rages. He tried his best to control himself during these attacks, but sometimes he

lost the ability to check himself. Whenever he began to get angry, his men knew the signs. They didn't know about the scar, but they were wary of his softened voice.

Cameron's hand dropped close to his gun butt.

"I said *enough,*" Slocum said. It was almost a whisper. His voice was very soft, with an upper-class Southern tinge to it. Once heard, it was never forgotten, as many people who had run across Slocum could testify.

"War's been over fifteen years, y'all," Bond said. Wells shrugged and slid the Winchester back into its scabbard. Slocum felt his head had stopped its throbbing. He sighed in relief, took a drink from his canteen, hooked it over his pommel and walked back to the railroad track. He took off his hat and kneeled again, as if he were a Moslem praying. But this time his acute hearing had picked up the infinitesimal vibration that signaled the coming of the train with its express car filled with gold ingots from the Dirty Dog mine. He rose with a thin smile, dusting his knees.

2

The arroyo—more of a barranca—had steep-walled sides rising up, almost vertically, for 80 feet. Two of the horses were hitched to dead cottonwoods, one was hitched to a mesquite. Slocum's horse, a five-year-old gray gelding, a well-trained cow pony, was standing patiently above his reins. Slocum had won him two months before in an all-night poker game in Tucson. There was one more horse. This was a sturdy packhorse; on his back he wore a packsaddle, designed for the gold ingots.

The barranca debouched into a broad valley. The 80-foot-tall walls curved around till they ran parallel to the railroad, 100 feet away. Huge boulders were embedded in the sloping sandstone. The four men had worked at undermining several of the largest with their picks, and now it was time to finish the job. Wells and Cameron clambered up, kicking a purchase into the soft soil with their pointed boots, and swung several times under the biggest boulders.

The boulders finally budged, began to slide and then somersaulted, gathering speed. Two ended against the near rail, and one large one, luckily, ended up between the rails. The engineer wouldn't see them until he rounded the bend 200 yards away, plenty of time to stop the train without damage.

He would not be alarmed. Such rock falls were common wherever the tracks came close to near-vertical cliffs, and every engine cab carried a crowbar to pry them out of the way.

The two men on the cliff slid down and ran into the barranca. Now everyone could hear the train wailing far across the valley. The tension was building. Everyone showed it, each in his way. Cameron began a horrible, tuneless whistling, Wells was breathing deeply and Bond began to scratch his nose. The tension affected Slocum differently. He squatted in the shade of his horse and began rolling a cigarette. Action acted upon him the way a lullaby affected children; it made him calm and relaxed. His mind functioned very well when it had to think fast. It was, perhaps, the quality that had made him a magnificent cavalry major in the war.

He licked the cigarette paper, pasted it, put it in his mouth and lit it. The three men looked at him in astonishment. He blew a long stream of blue smoke from his nostrils and met their stares.

"Got four minutes," he said.

"What's takin' that goddamn train?" demanded Cameron, pausing in his whistling.

"If you get in back of it an' keep blowin' like you are right now," said Wells, "it'll get here ninety-four miles an hour. For a fact."

"Goddamn you, you little squirt, shut your goddamn mouth!"

"When we finish this," observed Wells, "goddamnit effen I don't start a shoe factory on your fat ass."

"Let's go," Slocum said. He took one last drag on his cigarette, ground the butt into the dust until the last spark was killed and walked towards the tracks.

Wells came last, with his Winchester. His job was to cover them while they were in the train. All of them were tense except Slocum. His only worry was that Cameron might screw something up. He had never seen the man in action. Nothing seemed to be going right lately. But this two-chest shipment from the Dirty Dog would set him up nicely. He could use his share to take it easy in comfort while he carefully planned his next move. He thought of going down to Brazil where some ex-Confederate officers he knew were doing well.

He saw the engineer's tense face staring down at him from the engine cab. Slocum lifted a hand in casual greeting, as if he hadn't a care in the world.

3

"Good mornin'," Slocum said courteously. "We were headin' for Socorro and we came across these rocks. We figgered you'd need help gettin' 'em off the track. Got any crowbars?"

Steam hissed from the boiler. The engineer looked down. All that Slocum could see of the man was his head, as if he were crouching. There were no curious heads poking out of the windows of the single passenger coach.

Slocum did not like any of this. He had put together some expensively bought information: There would be two chests of ingots in the express car; there would be one guard in the car—a 63-year-old retired deputy sheriff with a reputation for cautious behavior. He had paid 200 dollars for this data and he was sure it was reliable.

But his sharp ears had caught the sound of horses stamping and leather creaking in the baggage car. Just as he turned to yell a warning, the baggage doors slid open. He dove headlong, yelling for them to scatter.

As soon as he hit the ground he rolled to one side. The sharp *crack!* of a carbine seemed to blend simultaneously with a spurt of dust where his prone body had been a scant second before. He came to his knees, firing at the open door of the baggage car, with a single shot at the engineer to make him think twice about joining in the firing. The bullet bounced off the iron with a loud clang. In the half-darkness of the inside of the baggage car, Slocum could make out the glint of several rifle barrels and the dark outlines of several saddled and bridled horses.

The corner of his right eye caught a movement in the engine cab. The engineer had ducked out of sight but surfaced again with a double-barreled shotgun. Slocum fired. His bullet smashed the breech. The engineer swore and dropped the gun, his hands tingling from the shock.

The roar of cartridge explosions mounted. Slocum flicked his eyes around. Wells had fired into the baggage car. He had hit one of the horses, as Slocum could tell from the shrill whinnying and plunging. Bond was calmly firing, forcing them to keep their heads low. Cameron was nowhere in sight.

"Keep shootin' an' pull back!" Slocum ordered. He rolled behind one of the boulders and squeezed off a shot. He wasn't trying to hit anyone. The rock near his head exploded into fragments and a small jagged piece of hot lead seared across his left cheek. The pain infuriated him. He stood up, aimed carefully and fired. Someone in the baggage car gasped with pain, took a step backwards, spun halfway around, lost his balance and tumbled onto the ground. He had been hit in the stomach.

Slocum ran forward in a crouch. He bent down, grabbed the man, pulled him to his feet and placed him across his shoulders in the fireman's carry. He set the muzzle of his Colt against the man's right hip and stepped boldly into full view.

The firing died down.

"Throw down the bullion!" he yelled.

No one moved.

"Throw it or I'll kill this sonofabitch!"

"There ain't none," the man he was carrying said weakly. "Put me down, mister. I hurt real bad."

Slocum paid no attention.

"You heard me," he said. "Throw it out or I'll blow a hole in him big enough for a blind man to piss through!"

He cocked the Colt.

The man groaned in agony.

"No bullion in here!" someone yelled in the darkness of the baggage car.

"He's tellin' the truth, mister," gasped the wounded man. "We knowed you'd be there, so we was all ready."

Slocum knew the man was telling the truth. No heads poking out of the passenger coach, the engineer crouching as he approached, the shotgun in the engine cab—it all added up.

He called out, "I'm takin' him with me! Anyone follow us, I'll kill 'im!" He hoisted the man more securely onto his shoulders, feeling sympathy for the man's groans, and walked slowly towards the barranca and the horses, keeping the Colt jammed into the man's ribs. No one stirred on the train.

There was no sound except the hissing of steam from the boiler, the panting of the wounded man and the sound of pebbles crunching underfoot as Slocum, Bond and Wells moved towards their horses. At that point Slocum became aware of two things simultaneously. Cameron was not in sight and Slocum's fine gelding was gone. He knew immediately that Cameron was the man who had betrayed them. And of course, Slocum knew why Cameron had suddenly taken to wearing bright red suspenders: it was because no one on the train would shoot him by mistake. The scar across Slocum's skull began to throb, as it always did when one of his rages was building.

As soon as they got clear, Slocum promised himself, he knew what his first piece of hard work would be. But that particular expenditure of cartridges would be a pleasure.

4

After three hours of hard riding towards the Apache country to the southwest, the prisoner's breathing became harsh and erratic. No dust clouds showed up behind them on the desert. Ahead loomed the jagged black sierra around which thunderstorms prowled like fat black wolves. It was a land of silence. The wounded man bent over his pommel, blood trickling from his mouth.

Slocum was riding doubled-up on Bond's horse, since it was the biggest. He dismounted and gently eased the man off and onto his back, under the sparse shade of an ocotillo. His face was gray.

Slocum's canteen had gone off with Cameron. He

took Bond's canteen and placed it beside the man. He would not be able to drink, but the water would cool his face. He unstrapped the blanket from the cantle and stretched it over the ocotillo branches to provide more shade.

Bond said quietly, "That ain't sensible, John. The man's gonna die right soon an' we're gonna need water and that blanket when we hit the mountains. I'm goddamn thirsty right now."

"If he's goin', I want him to go decent." Slocum's tone brooked no argument.

"Let 'im have it," Wells said. "I hear water is scarce in hell."

Slocum bent down. "We're leavin' you here," he said. "They'll be along in a few hours."

The three men mounted and rode on. Chalk up another one against Cameron, Slocum thought. If he hadn't betrayed them, the dying man wouldn't have been in the baggage car. Wells noticed Slocum's face. It was sunburned to a red-oak hue, his features were inexpressive and his green eyes were fixed on the black range ahead. A little pulse kept jumping nervously in his jaw.

Four more hours passed. They found a dry creek bed and explored up its rubble-strewn course for half an hour, but it was no use. Great gobs of foam oozed from their horses' mouthes and clung to the bits.

The men's tongues felt like pieces of wood. It was boiling hot and all the metal parts of their equipment were too hot to touch. They had drunk up all their water. The horses began to stumble. The mountains seemed as far away as ever.

Their mouths were so dry that they couldn't swallow their own sparse saliva. They had taken along plenty of rations in their saddlebags, but when Wells popped in a few chunks of brown sugar he was unable to dissolve them enough to swallow them. He spat them out in disgust.

Low sand hills stretched in every direction as far as they could see. They were barren of any vegetation, and the horses frequently sank to their knees in the loose white sand.

They had to get to the mountains for the water and shade. As for the Apaches who roamed there for exactly the same reasons, Slocum knew that Apaches in their right minds would never attack three well-armed, tough and experienced travelers. Slocum had shifted to Cameron's abandoned horse. He didn't like it; the man had disregarded all the rules of horse care. There were several large sores under the ragged saddle blanket.

"Hang me effen I didn't beat the whole Yankee army out of Kentucky," Wells suddenly said. Slocum understood that Wells was trying to keep their minds off their thirst. He nodded encouragingly.

"Yep," Wells went on, "I got away from the whole detail at Chattanooga with half a hog, a fifty-pound sack of flour, a jug of commissary whiskey and a camp kettle full of brown sugar."

"Stop talkin' 'bout vittles!" Bond snapped.

Wells looked at him coolly. "Now, take the biscuits my maw used to make, Bond," he went on, unconcerned. "They'd be just as light an' fluffy like dandelion puffs. They'd melt in yore mouth like a ripe Bartlett pear. You just pull 'em open—now, lissen, Bond, I think there's nothin' that shows a person's raisin' so well as to see him eat biscuits an' butter. Don' you agree?"

"Looka here——"

"Now, if he's been raised mos'ly on corn bread an' common doin's, an' don' know much 'bout good things to eat—like some people I know not more'n fifty miles from here—he'll mos' likely cut his biscuit open with a case knife an' make it fall flat as cow flop. But if he's used to biscuits, an' has had 'em often, he'll just pull 'em open, slow an' easylike, then he'll lay a little slice of fresh sweet butter, all cold from the well house, he'll lay it inside, then he'll drop a few drops of clear honey on this, an' stick the two halves back together again, an'——"

"Goddamnit, Wells, stop that nonsense or I'll go 'round you like a cooper round a barrel!"

Wells grinned. Suddenly sober, he went on. "I figgered somethin' was wrong when Cameron came peltin' up past me an' grabbed your pony, John. He said he was gonna come 'round onto the other side of the train, so I s'posed you told him to do it. He picked up your pony on those big Mex spurs he wears, an' shook him, an' when he set 'im down he was really runnin'. I could hear the rocks fallin' for minutes."

Wells mused for a second, licking his lips. Slocum noticed that the lips were cracked.

"If I'd'a knowed what he was up to," Wells added, "all I had to do was aim my Winchester right where them red suspenders crossed. Yep."

"We'll meet George again," Slocum said. His lips were pressed so tightly together that they showed only as a thin white streak.

An hour before dark they reached the foothills. The sand had disappeared. The going for the horses was much better, and the air had cooled off as they climbed upwards. The horses smelled water over a low ridge ahead. They were moving eagerly. The trail led past sagebrush, then piñons growing low among massive boulders. The ridge came closer to the trail. Then another ridge on the left edged closer to the trail. They were moving single file, in a *V* formed by the two ridges, their tongues swollen in their mouths, pushing hard for the water they knew the horses had smelled.

Suddenly rifle fire began. The narrow valley took the ear-piercing crashes and sent them bouncing back and forth. Wells was blown to one side, his head burst open like a ripe watermelon. Bond's horse had its right leg broken, and went down, floundering and whinnying. Its fall broke Bond's left thigh. One bullet seared deeply across the withers of Slocum's horse. It spun away from the source of the bullet so fast that its mane and tail flew in different directions. It spurted in huge bounds, quartering up the ridge at a speed Slocum would have never believed possible. It plunged between boulders, bucking wildly as it ran, and scraped under a piñon branch that jerked off Slocum's sombrero.

Another bullet passed between his arm and chest. By now Slocum was sure that they had not been ambushed by Apaches. The firing was too accurate. The final convincing argument for Slocum was the bullet that entered his back high on the right, broke his collarbone and exited, leaving a hole an inch across. The impact of the heavy bullet spun Slocum halfway to his left. He was almost at the crest of the ridge.

His horse stumbled. With his right arm useless Slocum could not keep his seat. He went over in a somersault. He could feel ribs breaking as he hit a pointed boulder with his chest. His horse regained its balance and kept running at full speed down the other side of the ridge. Slocum lay motionless. He could hear several horsemen spurring their horses up the ridge. He crawled several feet to one side and wedged himself between two steep-sided boulders. By now it was too dark for anyone to see the bloodstains he had left behind. He could feel the jagged edges of the broken ribs grinding together. He hoped to God his lungs were not punctured. He groped with his left hand for his Colt and withdrew it. He felt something was wrong with it. He looked down. The hammer had been snapped off somewhere in his wild somersault from his falling horse. He shoved it back inside the holster with a silent curse.

Five riders came over the ridge. Slocum could see them outlined against the dark blue sky. They were all white men and heavily armed. Slocum's horse was out of sight, but the five men could hear its hooves clattering among the loose stones far down the slope. They spurred in pursuit, riding only a few feet from where Slocum lay prone, pressing his left hand against his broken ribs and bleeding badly from his punctured shoulder.

As soon as they had gone by, he tore off the tail of his shirt and pressed it into and around the exit hole of the wound. He bound it into place with his bandanna. He knew he only had a few minutes before the pain would begin to immobilize him. He scrambled in and out of the boulders till only a bloodhound would be able to track him. Luckily the tight bandage prevented any blood from seeping through and dripping behind him.

Half an hour later, as the pain had started in his shoulder and chest, he heard the horsemen returning. They were walking their exhausted horses.

"Sonofabitch is jus' too fast, that's all," one of the men said. Even in his agony, Slocum permitted himself a thin smile. They hadn't realized they had been chasing a riderless horse, which, without the weight of a rider, could outrun anything except a thoroughbred.

"He ain't gonna get far," someone else said. Their voices carried clearly in the valley air. Slocum could see them all now as he looked downhill between two boulders. They all wore the deputy's star.

"Sheriff, what we do now?" one asked.

Andy Hamilton, a big, handsome redheaded man with a bull neck and fat thighs, spoke heavily. "He's headin' for Las Cruces. I'll telegraph 'em to watch for him. Or he's goin' further south, to El Paso, mebbe. Prob'ly he's headin' for Mexico till it gets quiet up here. One thing sure, he ain't goin' up into the mountains all by hisself. One man alone, why the 'paches'll fill 'im full of arrows like a porcupine, an' lift his hair besides."

"Mebbe he c'n squeeze by."

"Nope. He's got as much chance of doin' that as daylight has to get by a rooster. Nope. We'll get 'im Las Cruces way."

Their voices died away as they rode down to the trail. Slocum grimly pressed his bloodstained pad to stop the bleeding. It seemed to be getting worse. The pain had intensified. He decided to head deeper into Apache country. He had no weapon, no food, no horse, no water, no hat. He would wait till it was full dark, then he would move. The most important thing was to find water, right away.

The sun had sunk behind the western ridge. Down in the trail Wells lay dead. The deputies had taken his carbine and his gun belt, and torn open all his pockets looking for money. He had only three silver dollars. Bond's hands had been tied behind his back. They had made a rough splint for his broken thigh by lashing two dried piñon branches together with strips of fabric ripped from his pants leg. Three deputies stood over him. Slocum watched the sheriff dismount. He talked for a moment. The deputies showed astonishment. Some more deputies came up. Slocum counted them; there were 11 in all.

He put one hand over his chest and pressed against the broken ribs. Pain like jagged bolts of lightning ripped through him. He spat deliberately. There was no blood in the saliva, he saw. Thank God for that,

Slocum thought—they had not penetrated his lungs. He leaned back against a boulder and stared down at the men on the trail as they clustered about Bond.

He was sure he knew what had happened.

After Cameron had betrayed Slocum's plan for the holdup of the train, it was decided that Cameron should be present. Otherwise, Slocum would suspect something wrong and call it off. This would not be Cameron's idea, Slocum was sure. He was not a man who enjoyed taking risks. It had to be Hamilton's.

The idea for the red suspenders, then, would have to be his also. He would warn all the deputies not to fire at them. Smart man, the sheriff, Slocum thought. He looked forward to meeting him someday.

Then Hamilton, knowing Slocum's reputation for toughness and a general ability to wriggle out of any hazardous situation, decided that if their meeting at the train went wrong, Slocum would probably flee with his men to mountain country, with its water, unexplored valleys and hostile Apaches.

There would be no ranchers or settlers there willing to help out a sheriff with his posse, no one to tell him about the men he had seen riding by. Three well-armed, tough riders could protect themselves easily.

So, Slocum decided, Hamilton must have taken his deputies the night before the train left Socorro, swung out in a wide loop to the mountains so that Slocum would not come across the posse's tracks and then simply waited until Slocum and his exhausted men would ride between the two ridges.

Good strategy, Slocum thought. He had seen the sheriff before, in a restaurant in Socorro two months ago. He had contemptuously dismissed the man as a loud, boasting blowhard. He had now changed his mind. He wondered how much Cameron was getting for his betrayal. Slocum was wanted in Texas and the Nebraska Panhandle for bank robbery. There were reward posters tacked up in the Socorro post office. They had used drawings that did not look like him at all. The Cattlemen's Bank of Niobrara was offering 5,000 dollars, the Dakota National did not consider 10,000 too much for his body. The drawings were five years old. But the years in between had changed him. They had added several creases to his face and had given him some more crow's-feet at his eyes. And, Slocum thought, the artist would have been better employed as a street cleaner. But it was to his advantage, of course—the drawings bore hardly any resemblance to him. Slocum had tested them out by standing right next to them as he chatted with the postmaster, a sharp-eyed loquacious cripple who loved to reminisce about the Civil War. The man had not been in the least bit suspicious.

He watched the deputies bustling below. Someone brought up a horse. Several men hoisted Bond onto the saddle. Even at that distance in the growing dark Slocum could see Bond's face contort in silent agony. Unable to restrain himself, he uttered a low moan.

"It tickles, huh?"

The sheriff chuckled at his own joke.

"Water," Bond gasped.

"Gimme a canteen," the sheriff said. Someone handed him a canteen. He held it up to Bond's lips. As Bond leaned forward eagerly, the sheriff moved the canteen away two inches and slowly let it trickle out till it was empty.

Slocum slammed his clenched fist against a rock. It made a heavy thudding sound and for a second he thought they must have heard it down below. But no one looked up at him.

He thought the men would be leaving immediately. They would probably ride all night instead of sleeping right there. He began plotting a way to get Bond out of jail. He would need plenty, in case bribes would work. He would need two very good horses. He sat there, pressing his hand against his chest, planning. If the bribes didn't work out he knew a very good criminal lawyer in Santa Fe. He would need a very, very good one, since the man he had shot in the baggage car was likely dead. Tom Clark was very, very good, and knew how to get to the governor and the parole board. He would want at least 20,000 dollars. It was not unknown that a man could buy pardons in an election year when an incumbent usually needed plenty of money to run again. Slocum grinned: This was an election year. He felt a little better about the whole situation.

But to get the money Slocum would need other things first: a good doctor for himself who could be trusted to keep his mouth shut. He needed time to get well. Time to pick up two or three good men. Time to pick out a rich, little, unsuspecting bank. Time to case it thoroughly—Slocum's jobs always turned out well, because he took his time in preparation. And he needed time to get away. And time to get back to Santa Fe and Tom Clark.

All this, Slocum calculated, would take at the very least two months. Better count on four, Slocum told himself. A good lawyer could get delays. He would write a brief note to Tom Clark and tell him to get going—he had a good credit rating with Clark. The man would wait patiently for his money. Slocum began to feel better about it all.

But now he noticed that Bond's hands were not being tied to his saddle horn. They were left tied behind his back. Somone was leading his horse till it stopped under a tall piñon whose branches jutted out horizontally over the trail. Another deputy took his riata off his saddle. Suddenly Slocum knew what Hamilton was going to do.

He could do nothing. He watched in savage and

impotent rage as Hamilton took the riata, slipped the noose over Bond's neck, tossed the riata over the topmost branch, took the slack and made it fast to a lower branch. Then he slapped the horse's haunch with his open palm so hard that the crack sounded like a pistol shot.

The horse sprang forward like a jackrabbit. Bond was whipped out of the saddle. He began to sway back and forth only a few inches above the ground. The slipknot was too small to break his neck. He began to slowly strangle. His legs jerked and thrashed in the air.

It was taking too long for Hamilton's satisfaction. He walked over, grabbed both legs—Slocum gritted his teeth as he imagined the added agony of the broken thigh—squeezed them together and hung all his weight on Bond's torso. The thrashing stopped. After three minutes Hamilton released the legs. The body was motionless. Hamilton went through Bond's pockets. He would find nothing, Slocum knew. They had all been just about penniless. The deputy whose riata had been used did not want it back.

The men mounted and rode away. The moon began to rise above the barren ridge back of Slocum. He did not move. The bleeding did not stop. He felt dizzy. He stood up, weaved, took one step and fell. He tried again and fell again. He began to crawl downhill towards the trail. By the time he reached it his trousers were shredded and his knees were scraped raw. He noticed that the blood was dripping faster and faster from his shoulder. He reached the trail and found a dead branch. Using it as a crutch, he forced himself upright and began a slow ascent along the trail.

Slocum was a bad enemy. When he had come back from the war he found his home in ashes, with only the old brick chimney left standing. He had had no leave for four years. When the Northern troops rode through, Slocum's father fired at them from the upstairs window. They hung the 65-year-old man from the chinaberry tree in the yard, looted the house of all its silver cutlery and then set fire to it. This was in January. His mother died of pneumonia from the exposure to the chilly rain that fell that night. Two years later Slocum found the captain who had commanded that troop. The man lived in upstate New York. Slocum called him to the door of his house, told the man and his wife who he was and why he was there, and then shot and killed the ex-captain.

To reclaim his ancestral property was, by that act, impossible. So he rode west, where eastern warrants did not seem to interest anyone.

Slocum fainted again. When he was unconscious his old nightmare began again: His father was hanging from the chinaberry tree, trying to say good-bye to his wife. She kept screaming. The captain pushed her away roughly. She bit his hand. He called her a rebel bitch and pushed so hard that she stumbled and fell. All this had happened, as Slocum had found out from the house servants. In the nightmare he was riding hard at the head of his patrol, and each time he almost made it to the chinaberry tree in time to cut his father down, scatter the bluebellies, save his father's life and stamp out the fire that had just been set. But each time he dreamed, he awoke almost at the gate of the yard, sweating and trembling. His anguish had not lessened with the passing years.

The nightmare this time was especially vivid. He was bent low over his horse's neck, and he could see the blue uniforms clustered around the chinaberry. His horse gathered himself for a leap over the fence. The jump would put Slocum spang in the middle of the bluebellies. Slocum felt exultant and began to yell, but his horse got himself tangled in the top rail and fell on his side with Slocum underneath. The men began to hoist his father. He would not be able to save him.

In the dream he began weeping with despair.

5

Slocum awoke from his nightmare. His side and his shoulder hurt badly. Nevertheless he felt relief, as he always did when he realized it was only a dream.

Light splattered down on him. It was daylight. He had lain in the trail all night, he thought, and he was interested at discovering that he was no longer thirsty. For some time he could not understand why the light seemed to filter down on him in irregular patterns.

He turned his head to one side.

He saw two dark brown hands with heavy silver bracelets. The hands were clasped together. He knew they were the hands of an Indian. His mind flashed the word *Apache!* and he automatically dropped his hand down to his hip for his Colt, but somehow he could not move his arm. He looked down and saw that the arm was tied to his side. He tried to sit up, but the pain in his chest and shoulder flooded him in an agonizing rush.

One of the brown hands pushed him gently back. He saw it was a woman's hand. A voice spoke. Slocum turned his head and saw a figure outlined against a brilliant turquoise sky. It had hair down to its shoulders. Surmounting it was a set of deer antlers. For a second Slocum thought it was a medicine man, but the figure set down its carbine and let the deer carcass slide off his wide shoulders.

The man and the woman spoke. Slocum recognized

the harsh sibilance of Apache. He was lying on a pile of deerskins. He was in a jacal. The branches laid across the few upright members made the light pattern that had so puzzled him when he woke up.

He seemed to be in no immediate danger. He licked his lips. They felt caked and dry. The woman, who was sitting cross-legged beside the deerskins, bent forward, dipped an old cotton rag into a gourd full of cool water and placed a corner of the damp rag in Slocum's mouth. He gratefully chewed it, delighting in the drops that trickled slowly down his throat.

He watched the man hang the deer by its hocks to a piñon branch near the jacal. He began to skin it. Slocum heard children's voices as they splashed in a river nearby. Flies buzzed near the deer offal. It sounded very calm and peaceful. He fell asleep.

Later he woke up. The woman was patting his face. It was a nice way to be waked up, Slocum thought. She had made a venison stew with corn. She fed him from a small gourd with a big silver spoon. He felt much better. The man was sitting cross-legged, smoking a cigarette and watching him calmly. He saw that Slocum was coherent. He hitched closer.

"You better," he said. He had a deep voice. He had a broad, flat face, colored deep reddish-brown, and black eyes. His shoulders were enormous.

"How long have I been here?"

"Mebbe three weeks." He turned and spoke to the woman.

She bent down and unwound the bandage around his shoulder. Slocum saw it was a new one, made from a red cotton fabric. The exit hole had almost closed. The skin was pink and healthy. The entrance wound, as he saw by twisting his head, was closed. The skin looked good. There was no inflammation. She took some dried leaves from a buckskin pouch, mixed them with a little grease from a small gourd and rubbed the mix into the entrance and exit wounds. Then she bandaged him again.

Slocum tested his chest by taking a deep breath. There was no pain.

"You had bones broke there," the man said. "Also shoulder broke. OK now."

It was true. The ribs had healed. He felt along his right collarbone. It felt smooth. It had healed perfectly. He ran a finger over the greasy bandage and smelled it.

"Bear fat. Good for you."

"Why didn't you kill me?"

The man shrugged. "Her son killed four moons ago. She cried all the time. She saw you and want you for son."

Slocum turned and looked at her. She was engaged in cutting the venison into strips and hanging them over a crude rack to dry in the sun. She was much heavier than his mother. Her hands were bloody and she wiped them from time to time on her long purple velveteen skirt. It was filthy, smeared with grease and smoke. Her calloused feet were bare. Her long, black hair, liberally sprinkled with gray, hung down her back.

"Oh, she heap savvy you!" the man said.

Slocum watched her. Her brown square hands were swift and competent as she sliced the venison.

"You fight her, you fight me. You hurt bad. We tie you down. You curse us bad."

She looked up and saw Slocum staring at her. She looked at him in a cool level stare.

"She got no husband, no son. She my aunt. Her name Idizhode."

At the sound of her name Idizhode smiled.

"It mean 'lightning'. When she a girl she slap men's faces real fast when they touch her."

Slocum liked her. He suddenly felt tired. It was cool under the branches. He fell asleep.

6

A week later Slocum was able to sit up. The wounds had closed perfectly. Next he tried to stand. His legs could not support him. He had lost 30 pounds. He could feed himself. When he ate he averted his eyes from the drying venison. The strips were covered solidly with small black flies with beautiful golden heads. But the venison stew was tasty. There was also coffee.

Every day he tried walking a little. It was hard, and he began to sweat after a few steps, but every day he managed to stay on his legs a little longer. His right arm had lost a lot of its strength.

Between the long spells of unconsciousness he had heard the shouts and screams of children. The sound floated upwards through a grove of cottonwood trees. One day, after he had been with the Apaches for five weeks, he walked slowly, supporting himself on a stick, all the way to the grove. He sat on a log, panting and sweating, but happy at his accomplishment. A creek came out of the mountain to the west, meandered across a valley over a shallow pebbled bottom and then, warmed by the sun as it slid over the shallows, widened into a pool fringed with tall grasses.

Most of the naked children splashed and swam there. A band of Warm Springs Apache had just come to visit and gather piñon nuts. Slocum was too shy to join them. He waited till the children felt the tug of hunger and ran screaming through the grove and up to their mothers. He stripped and waded into the cool water and launched himself gingerly. There was no current to fight against. He swam back and forth a few times, exercising his wasted shoulder muscles. In a few minutes he was exhausted. He swam out and lay on the bank drying in the sun.

In a week he was swimming back and forth for much longer periods. His right shoulder was getting stronger. For the first time in his life his entire body was tanning. One afternoon when a breeze was blowing he could hear the children coming back. He sat up, and as he was pulling on his trousers he suddenly saw green paper fluttering above the group.

One piece drifted above him and settled down in the tall grass. Idly, he reached over. It was a $20 treasury bill. He leaped to his feet without bothering to put on his shirt. By the time he had finished he had picked up 37 more, caught in the grass or floating in the water. He dried the wet ones in the sun. He hid them in a tin can he found in the camp's rubbish.

The next morning, at sunrise, Nachodise, the man with the wide shoulders, took him hunting. Nachodise said the exercise would be good for him. Besides, he would have to learn Apache ways. Slocum agreed. He would not go back to Socorro unless he was in perfect condition. On the way to the hunting grounds they walked through the Warm Springs camp. The chattering of the children and the camp noises stilled as they stared at him. They had heard about the adoption, and no one made any hostile gestures. Moreover, they were afraid of Nachodise. One girl came out of her jacal, half bent over, and for a fraction of a second, framed by her long blue-black hair, Slocum could see her firm breasts quivering under the open neck of her deerskin dress.

He had not thought of women for months, but the sight made his penis swell with excitement. He stopped for a moment and stared at her as she straightened up. She knew he was interested. Her black eyes stared boldly back at him.

She was five and half feet tall, taller than the usual Apache girl. She set down a large gourd in which she had prepared the soapy water of sotol stalks, and as he stared she bunched her long hair with both hands and thrust it into the water. Her long brown fingers firmly kneaded the hair.

Slocum imagined her fingers caressing his thighs and edging slowly towards his swollen penis. He swallowed.

Her head came up. Her hair was piled in a solid mass that shone like wet, black marble. Her arms, lifted and kneading her hair, thrust her breasts forward. She knew Slocum was staring. She pretended to yawn and stretched her arms wide. Slocum saw the hard, small protuberances formed by her nipples under the supple deerskin. Oh, my God, Slocum thought, I've got to have that girl.

Nachodise pushed him. He tore his eyes away and followed the Apache through the encampment.

Nachodise spoke. "Kids say you took green paper."

There was no way out of it. Slocum nodded.

"No good to us."

A few months ago, Nachodise told him, a Chiricahua war party had cut off a paymaster and his escort. They didn't know what the green stuff was. There was no demand for it. Even if they knew what it was, no one would want it. Silver dollars had real metal, could be buried, or could be taken to the Navajos, who would make bracelets or necklaces out of them. But paper money rotted if it was buried. Or the mice would gnaw it to shreds. Nachodise did not ask for it.

He wore elk-hide moccasins. They made no sound. Slocum kept breaking sagebrush twigs under his soles. He had an old Henry Nachodise had lent him, and the ring on the stock kept rattling. Nachodise stopped and made Slocum wrap it with a length of sinew. Slocum carried a canteen that Nachodise had taken away years ago from a cavalryman. He stopped long enough to take a couple of swallows, and when he finished he had to run to catch up.

When they were trotting together, Nachodise pointed out that the water was sloshing around in the canteen and making too much noise. Deer heard very well. Slocum offered Nachodise a drink but he refused. Slocum drank it all.

By the time the sun had cleared the eastern horizon and had burned off the dew, they had trotted six miles. Slocum was panting like a dog but his second wind was coming. Nachodise touched his arm and pointed. Four hundred yards ahead, broadside on, standing on a lava ridge, was a doe.

Slocum hadn't fired a shot since the day of the attempt on the train. Never, since his father first trained him to handle a gun when he was eight, had he ever passed such a lengthy period without firing at game or at a man. As he brought up the rifle he felt very tense. Had he lost his markmanship? Nachodise had refused to let him practice at a target. Cartridges were too scarce and too expensive. Slocum had cleaned it and sighted it; he had practiced snap-firing with it until his arm and shoulder muscles ached—but how did she throw? Too high? To the left? To the right?

Now the doe stood motionless. He felt a breeze on his right cheek. He allowed for the bullet's drift, set his sight, pressed the stock against his cheek and squeezed the trigger.

The doe leaped, took three quick steps and fell. Slocum felt so relieved that he disregarded the pain caused to his newly healed collarbone by the heavy recoil. Now he knew he could go back to Socorro looking for Cameron and Hamilton and not worry about his muscular coordination.

He turned to Nachodise with a happy smile.

"How's *that?*" he demanded.

"*You* carry 'im back," Nachodise replied.

7

Slocum watched Idizhode as he ate. She was trying to teach him Apache. She was enormously pleased when he set down two deer haunches in front of her jacal. He felt proud that he was now able to repay her somewhat for the care she had given him. She had saved his life, and there was absurdly little he could do to repay her. She had massaged his right shoulder every night, smiling that there was now a man in her jacal, strong and able to take care of her. But when he thought that he was getting ready to leave her as soon as he could travel, he felt ashamed. What could he say to her? He felt ashamed.

After he ate he tried to sleep. It was impossible. He slipped out and walked slowly to the cottonwood grove. It was an uncommonly warm day for that altitude, and he felt the sweat trickling down his back. The children were off on the piñon slopes with their parents, clubbing the branches and knocking down the ripened nuts. He could hear their sharp, jubilant voices across the valley.

Under the interlocking tall branches of the cottonwoods it was cool. He stripped and stepped knee-deep in the cool green water with a sigh of pleasure.

In front of him the surface of the water stirred and swelled upwards. A shining black mass broke into the air. For a second Slocum thought it was a beaver, but beavers were brown. Was it a black bear? He spun and splashed quickly towards the shore.

Rich female laughter pealed behind him. He halted and turned. It was Idagalele—he had found out her name from Nachodise. She was kneeling on the bottom. The water came to her neck. In gestures she told him she had seen him coming, had hidden in the tall grass to one side, and when he had entered the water she had slipped underneath and swam in a curve till she was heading directly for him.

He stared at her. She was serenely aware of it. She twisted her floating hair into one braid and pulled it high in the air. The movement lifted her breasts. The faint chill of the water had hardened her nipples till they perched on the tips of her breasts like small acorns. She began to twist her braided hair; the working of her arms and shoulders forced her breasts to quiver.

Slocum knew his penis was swelling. She stared at it calmly and frankly, not at all in the half-hypocritical, half-excited manner of most of the white women he had known who were not prostitutes; nor did she look at him in the bored, cool manner of the whores of the cow-town cribs.

He moved into deeper water. She slowly rose to a standing position and moved slowly backward till the water reached her waist. Slocum advanced towards her, his heart beating with excitement. She remained still. He moved closer till he felt her stiff nipples touch his chest. She smiled and began to move her torso from side to side. Her nipples brushed against him with a feather-light touch. He lifted his arms and she slid backwards till she stood in water up to her neck. He followed.

The water flowed around him like blue silk. Her hair had slid out of its loose braid and floated around her head in a black, supple, sinuous cloud. She waited serenely.

Her arms came up, slid past his hips, went down, stroked his buttocks, and then her palms slid around to his groin. One palm cupped his testicles, the other gripped his hard penis, relaxed and then stroked it gently. His arms went around Idagalele and pressed her hard against him.

She rubbed her breasts against his chest. He was breathing fast, and she, using the water as an oil, was sliding around him, teasing him, her hands cleverly stroking his thighs and his genitals and varying the pressure. She came around to face him. He bent down and kissed her. Her breath was fragrant, redolent of the crushed wood fiber with which she cleaned her teeth. She forced his lips apart with her fingers, put her tongue inside his mouth and flicked it in and out.

They waded ashore. Spreading their clothes on the dried leaves under a thick tangle of branches they kneeled down together. She pushed him gently onto his back. Her mouth came down on his fiercely. Her passion surprised him. Her mouth slid down to his neck, his chest, his stomach, and slowly came to his penis. His arms reached out and cupped her hard breasts. He had never been so aroused in his life.

During the rest of the afternoon they made love three times.

Two days later he saw her sitting cross-legged in front of her jacal. She had pegged out a deerskin and was cutting into it. He stopped and watched her movements. They were quick and sure, without any wasted motion. She looked up at him. He liked the way she looked at him: frankly, without any coquetry. She dropped her glance to his genitals and his penis instantly hardened. She stared at the bulge calmly. She pointed to the sun, traced its course through the sky with a forefinger all the way to its setting, shaped a half-moon with both hands, and pointed to a place in the night sky. Then she pointed to his penis and smiled.

Slocum was delighted and somewhat embarrassed.

He was still not accustomed to the complete sexual frankness of Indian women.

By now she had cut out a section of deerskin. She folded it quickly. Slocum saw it was going to be a small pouch. She made signs saying it would be his. He was touched. The small gourd beside her was half-full of the small blue glass beads she would use for decoration. He bent down and traced the letter *S* on the pouch and pointed to the beads. She understood immediately and nodded, with a flash of brilliant white teeth.

That night she came to the grove.

8

The full moon came. It was time for Slocum to go. With a sharp knife Idizhode had given him, he trimmed his mustache and beard. With his cleaned-up and neatly stitched pants, an old shirt, an old sombrero Nachodise had given him, his old, worn boots, a sisal morral filled with dried jerky and the tin can of money, he looked the way he wanted to: like a miner out of work.

His canteen was slung over one shoulder and the knife was strapped to his belt. He had gotten up at three, when the moon was soaring up over the western ridge. He had not said good-bye to anyone. He hated good-byes and he felt guilty about leaving so abruptly. He felt badly about leaving before Idagalele finished his pouch with his initial on it. At least he had learned something from Nachodise: He walked in his stocking feet for a quarter of a mile before he stopped to put on his shoes.

It was too dangerous traveling in Apache country on the trails. He took to the ridges, striking out south-east, heading for Silver City. He had no blankets nor did he dare make a fire. He lived on the jerky and upland springs. He had no blankets, but it was warm enough during the days when he slept under the pines. One morning, just before sunrise, he came to a water hole. It was still muddy. It had been riled up by mounted Indians. Being wary, Slocum had carefully kept in the shelter of the pines on the ridge crest while he reconnoitered. He spotted eight of them, smeared all over with dried mud. They blended into the dried soil beside the road as they lay flat, waiting for anyone who might come along the trail. He swung around in a wide loop, crossed over the ridge and made his way with great difficulty through acre after acre of trees leveled in a long-ago thunderstorm. Hours later he emerged once more on the ridge top. From there he saw the shacks and mine shafts of Silver City sprawling up and down the hillside. He moved down to the road and plodded into the town, wan and exhausted. He found a restaurant and sat down on a kitchen chair. It was the first chair he had sat on for two months and it seemed unnatural to sit on it rather than sit on the floor with his legs outstretched.

"Can I get lunch?" he asked the unshaven waiter.

"Lunch, hell! The next meal is supper an' you'll git it 'bout six if we have any luck."

Slocum fell asleep on the chair. He slept for three hours. The waiter prodded him awake.

He ate a big slice of fried ham with plenty of rich brown gravy, ten fluffy biscuits, big baked Irish potatoes and a pot of coffee.

"Good, eh?" demanded the waiter. "Looks like your big intestines went an' ate up your little intestines. Been starvin'?"

"Yep. Lookin' for work here an' there."

"Minin'?"

"Yep."

"Nothin' much doin'. Mines gettin' played out. Where you comin' from?"

This had to be expected.

"From Nevada way."

"By God. That's damn far, that is! See any 'paches?"

"No."

"We got a couple cavalry patrols 'round here. No damn good! March eighteen miles a day, with lobster an' gingerbread doin's, an' applesass, an' think they'll ketch 'paches as rides eighty miles a day and thinks nuthin' of it!"

"Yep. Think I'll look 'round, anyway."

He got a shave and took a hot bath in a room back of the barbershop. As he lay soaking in the big zinc tub he planned his next moves. The plot looked fine. He dressed, walked across the street to a haberdashery, and bought three white linen shirts, a black vest, black coat and trousers, black leather half boots, a narrow-brimmed black felt hat and underwear. Slocum was going to be a gambler.

He walked down the street to a gunsmith's. The owner, a sharp little man with black eyes, was repairing a shotgun while his customer was waiting. As Slocum walked in the customer said, "Tell ye how I felt 'bout the Confederacy. I killed a power of 'em. Times I wished the hull dang thing was hangin' over hell by just one string. Oh, I wished I had a knife, I'd just slash it!"

Slocum stared at him. He ordered a double-barreled derringer for nighttime wear, a Colt .45 and ammunition for both weapons. He considered staying and getting into a conversation with the man with the shotgun, but he regretfully came to the decision that it would be better to avoid any friction. He nodded and left. He went back to the hotel, slept for several hours, awoke refreshed, took a bath and a shave, dressed and threw away his old clothes.

He walked slowly down the street. He felt pleased. Three years he had been in Silver City—and neither the gunsmith nor the haberdasher had recognized him. True, he had a mustache then, and the years had put lines on his face. He entered the Miner's Daughter saloon, bought some cigars and headed directly for the poker tables. He picked the one that had the biggest piles of chips stacked on it.

He watched the players' styles, smoking silently. After an hour one of the miners said in a disgusted tone, "Aw, the hell with it!" The man rose.

"Mind if I sit in?" Slocum asked. No one objected. He sat down and bought a hundred dollars' worth of chips with greenbacks.

Slocum never gambled. He played cards honestly, but he did not gamble. He watched his opponents very carefully. He noted how they bid, how they raised, and he watched their cards. He observed the cards they displayed after each round. He tied that up with their expressions as they received their cards; with their expressions as they raised and called. Thus he learned quickly what credence to give to their bids and bluffs when he would be playing against them. He particularly watched their eyes.

Most men, he knew, had control over their faces. But they could not control the involuntary movements of their eyes. When the cards were being dealt, Slocum never looked at his right away. He watched his opponents' faces and eyes. Only after had that information been filed away in his memory did he look at his hand.

So whenever he saw an eye movement indicating delighted surprise, and when his cards were not very good, Slocum calmly dropped out. He did not consider what he was doing to be gambling. It was hard, exhausting, skilled labor.

He played until 2 A.M. He walked away from the table $360 richer. He was too restless to sleep. He sat up all night by his window, smoking and thinking that he would have to be very careful about getting close to Cameron and Hamilton. It would be important to practice his old skills. In the morning as soon as the bank opened, he got himself a bankbook in the name of Samuel Sheridan. He liked the idea of choosing his names after Northern generals.

He rented a horse in a livery stable and rode out to a small level area close to the town. He set up empty whiskey flasks on fence posts and practiced daily with the Colt. Standing, walking, running, riding. He practiced quick draw, but he never fired for speed at the expense of accuracy. He preferred to be a second slower than the man shooting at him. Better that than to get his gun out first and then miss.

He stripped to his undershorts afterwards and ran up and down the flats. The first day he ran for five minutes. The second day for ten, the third for fifteen and so on.

By the end of three weeks he knew he was in top physical condition. His aim was excellent, he had placed $1750 in the bank, and he had acquired a reputation as a cool, professional gambler, whose lifestyle bore no resemblance at all to the *Man Wanted* poster for a heavily mustached John Slocum. He saw the poster every time he walked by the post office.

People called him Mr. Sheridan. He was always courteous, paid his bills promptly in cash, and he always made it a point to play with cowmen and salesmen passing through Silver City. He wanted his reputation to precede him to Socorro.

One night he played with two ranchers from the rolling plain country southwest of Albuquerque. They were chatting about the recent attempt on the train.

One of them, a well-educated Texan, had heard the full story from a deputy on Hamilton's posse.

"One of the robbers," he said, through a cloud of cigar smoke, "was hanged under painful circumstances. His executioners were without experience."

The men at the table chuckled. Slocum forced a thin smile to his lips. It was now the end of his fourth week in Silver City.

It was time to put his plan into operation.

9

Next morning he took the twice-weekly stagecoach to Deming. He waited one day and took the next stage for Las Cruces. He arrived covered with the white dust of the trail, shaken up the wretched springs and the rut-filled road. He got out at Las Cruces, stretched himself out on a bench outside the stage office, and wondered how the women who rode them could possibly survive. After half an hour he rose and bought a ticket on the train for Socorro.

There would be a train next morning. He was too tense to sleep. There would be no point taking a hotel room in his state, and Slocum knew it. He sat all night in the railroad depot, smoking and staring at the floor. The stationmaster came in at 11 to tell him he would have to get out till the morning, but one look at the icy-green eyes that lifted to look at him was enough. The stationmaster decided discretion was the better part of valor and withdrew without saying anything. When he opened the door in the morning the room was thick with tobacco smoke and Slocum didn't even bother to look at him. The stationmaster knew that Slocum had lifted his head, but the eyes were staring past him, fixed on something. Whatever they were fixed on, thought the stationmaster, he was glad he was not on the receiving end. Slocum's face was unshaven and hard as a rock. He was thinking over what his colonel had once told him during the war. "John, everywhere this is the way of war; lie still and lie still. Then up and maneuver and march hard; then a big battle and then a lot more lie still."

Well, Slocum thought, he was about to start a war; he had had enough of lying still. The train came in the station. He hoisted his carpetbag onto his shoulder and got on the train. The stationmaster was glad to see him leave.

Socorro was a sleepy Mexican town that had allowed the American occupation to slide over it with a resigned shrug. It sat placidly beside the brown river and passively watched the Anglo ranchers and their cowboys ride in, make their purchases, get drunk, get laid, shoot each other and ride out, sometimes no farther than the cemetery at the edge of town. There were cattle-holding pens beside the railroad, and a lot of cattle got shipped out on the cattle cars, and a lot of money came into Socorro.

Since there was a lot of money, it acted as honey to attract those three flies that always cluster around money: banks, brothels and bars. A lot of people came in to look for money. Some stayed and opened businesses, some stayed in the cemetery and some went out again.

Slocum knew it well.

But when he swung off the train, he stood for a while, taking it all in just as if he had never seen it before. He smoked an inch off his cigar, leisurely surveying the town. Then he picked up his bag and strode across the street, as if he had finally picked out his hotel. It was the Texas Star, the biggest hotel in Socorro—and the one where he had stayed in his previous visits.

He entered, put the bag down and tapped the tarnished bell beside the register. Old Henry Tompkins came shuffling out of his little room where he always sat playing solitaire. He was a wizened little man with a gray stubble on his face and wisps of gray hair floating around his bald head. This would be the acid test. If Tompkins didn't recognize him, Slocum's chances of staying alive in Socorro would be good.

Slocum looked very different than he had two months ago. His heavy mustache was gone. That alone was an enormous change, along with the cleanly shaven face that before had a perennial two-week growth. His hair was neatly trimmed; before his hair had curled over his shirt collar. He had lost 20 pounds. His face was pale because of all the time he had been spending inside saloons, and slightly drawn, almost a little dissipated. That was good; he intended to stay out of the sun. Before he had been sunburned and very brown because of the constant exposure to the range and desert sun. He had been surprised to find several gray hairs falling onto the barber's dirty apron in Silver City; when he looked into his first mirror in months he saw that his hair was sprinkled with more gray hairs. He had practiced talking in a quick, nervous flat Northern accent while he was in Silver City instead of his soft Southern speech; people had accepted that right away, and several had asked if he came from Connecticut. Yes, Slocum thought, he stood a good chance of getting away with it.

Tompkins stood there in his old carpet slippers. He pulled up his suspenders and hooked them over his shoulders. This was his way of dressing up for guests.

"Morning," Slocum said pleasantly. "Might I have a room?"

Tompkins grunted. He snapped each suspender. Then he looked at the register.

"Yup. Three dollars a night."

"I'd like it by the week."

"Plannin' on hangin' 'round a bit?"

"Yes."

"Ummm. That'll cost yuh twenty-one dollars."

"I thought there might be a reduction."

"Thought wrong. Twenty-one. In advance."

In his best Northern accent, Slocum said calmly, "Isn't that a bit unusual, sir?"

"You whippersnapper, I smelled gambler a mile off when I seen you! They come as popular in my hotel like a rattler in dog town. You pays in advance or you kin bed down in the liv'ry stable. What'll yuh have?"

Slocum chuckled silently. He was pleased that he had managed to fool Tompkins. He paid his $21, signed the register "Samuel Sheridan, Cheyenne," and asked the old man why he was so hard on gamblers.

"Tell yuh why, sonny. Many's the time one of 'em's been playin' monte or stud. An' some cowboy finds out the gambler's been holdin' an extra ace up his sleeve for emergencies like. Why, then, they exchange words and usually lead. An' then they cart off the gambler to the bone orchard and here he is owin' me back rent. At least the undertaker gits paid for the coffin by the county. I don't git a penny. Nothin' personal, sonny."

"Of course not. Looks like a lively town."

"Yep. They got somethin' new here, a vigilante committee which is very vigilant. Besides hangin' a man ever' week or so, they come 'round every evenin' an' collect two bucks fer each table 'fore they let the games open. Sheriff don' do nothin'. Never seen nothin' like it, an' I been to Tascosa, been to Ogalalla, I been in Frisco in '49."

Slocum wanted to hear more about the sheriff but he decided to play it slow and easy.

"That's a long time ago."

"Yep. There's nothin' hardly legal 'bout this town. Ah, the hell with it. Where was I? Yup. Back in '49

I jumped ship an' headed for the diggin's. Made myself a buckskin sack to hold the gold. I was pretty handy with a needle. I made it the size of a pillowcase. When I found some dust I seed the bag was too big. So I cut it down a bit. An' next crick I was lucky in, well, I cut it down some more. An' next time I struck it decent, I was in the south fork of the American River, an' this time it was as big as a Bull Durham sack, an' that time I was sensible."

"You're certainly an old-timer."

"Been around since the year one. Only the mountains been here longer."

Slocum nodded. He offered a cigar to the old man.

"Thank 'ee kindly."

Slocum lit it. "Never heard of vigilantes runnin' games," he said.

"Never did neither," Tompkins retorted.

"Sheriff no good?"

"Ain't that. Seen better. Seen worse. But who's gonna say anythin' 'gainst vigilantes? An' they're pickin' up nice money. There's eighty-seven tables in town. That's a hundred seventy-four dollars a night. In seven days, that's twelve hunnert eighteen dollars. Damn good. What do they do with it?"

"Pension off old vigilantes?"

"Nothin' to joke 'bout," Tompkins said, disgusted. "I bet you a poke of the best Snake River dust most of it's goin' into Hamilton's jeans."

"Who's Hamilton?"

"The sheriff."

"Nice."

"Nice is right! He's not doin' any graftin' personal, right? He's not goin' 'round extortin', right? Every week someone meets him somewhere an' gives him a bag full of silver dollars. He sure don't bank it. He's makin' a good thing out of bein' sheriff. Goddamn!"

Tompkins chewed his cigar, fuming.

"Know how big that bag is?" he demanded. "Big as the one I made when I first hit the diggin's. An' he *needs* it. He's got a brand-new wife. Cute as a speckled pup under a red wagon."

"Ah?" said Slocum, intrigued. This was interesting.

"Yep. Rich li'l gal. Met her back east, he did. She jus' come out a month ago. Very uppity. He's goin' to build a house she'll like, he says. A grand pianner come out with her. I heard 'er playin' on it."

Slocum was more interested. Another idea had begun to form. He liked the idea of the sheriff's collecting all that graft. He couldn't complain publicly if it were removed from him. And now that he had a pretty new wife—oh, it could become very interesting to see Hamilton's face if he woke up one morning and found her gone, too.

Things were looking up.

"Don' like the way she plays," Tompkins was saying. "They got a perfesser playin' the pianner in the Texas Star. She said he plays like a gorilla with gloves on. He plays damn good. I like fer a man to get both shoulders and all them back muscles into action playin' like the perfesser. She plays them awful sissy tunes. A feller can't whistle to 'em. The sheriff don't say nothin'. He likes everythin' she does. You oughta see that white lace dress she wears on Sundays. Wooooeeee! Ching Yee says it come all the way from Paris, France."

"Ching Yee?"

"The laundryman. When he irons that dress he says she stands right over 'im like a rattler coilin' hisself in front of a pack rat. Makes him nervous. He don't like it much, but no one likes to tangle with Hamilton."

Slocum went slowly up the stairs, smoking and thinking hard. Tompkins hadn't recognized him, not even after their long conversation. The room hadn't changed. It was separated from the next one by a partition of rough, unmatched pine. There were strips of cloth over the larger cracks. The ceiling had been once painted white. It was now a smoky yellow. The wallpaper was broken by warping. Large patches were missing. Cobwebs stretched wherever two walls met. Rough cotton sheets covered the thin cotton mattress. Both were clean enough. There was a high-post bedstead and one cane-seat chair. A small mirror hung on the wall. There was a small bureau. He emptied out his carpetbag of the few items. On a small table stood a cracked washbowl and a pitcher without a handle. Several pieces of carpet managed to cover the floor pretty well. Slocum had seen worse.

He lay down on the bed, kicked off his boots, clasped his hands behind his head and smoked quietly.

Things looked better, he decided. Hamilton looked to be in love with his wife. Oh, that was very good.

He stubbed out his cigar on the scarred little bedside table. He needed rest before the evening's work, which would have to give him enough background on the town so that he would be able to flesh out the bare bones of his plan for revenge.

10

Slocum woke at eight. He had the ability to get up almost at the minute he wished, and when he did so he was always wide awake and alert as a fox, no matter how exhausted he was. He washed his face and combed his hair in the mirror. He never looked at himself in the mirror, really. He looked to see if his hair were neat, and so forth. If he had taken a careful, self-evaluating stare, he would have seen a hard-featured man with a curious, tired expression in his eyes. He was tired of being forever on guard and tired with the realization he would never be able to relax a second as long as he would be in Socorro.

He slid his derringer from under the pillow. He put it in his right coat pocket. The heavy fabric would not betray its presence.

He walked downstairs, nodded to Tompkins and walked into the street. Socorro was a hard, sweaty little town. Its detractors in Santa Fe said it was "a thousand miles from nowhere, all booze, brothels, cattle, cards and six-guns, and just across the Rio Grande." And now that the respectable women had gone home and the kids were in bed, there was nothing to restrain anyone from doing just what he wanted.

Cowpunchers were spurring their ponies up and down the street in suddenly arranged races. Others were retching their guts out in the alleys back of the saloons where they wouldn't be stepped on by the horses. It was a rich, mean little cow town, and anything went as long as the local people weren't shot or the respectable women not annoyed. And there was no need for that, since Socorro had the biggest red-light district south of Albuquerque; nothing compared with it till El Paso. It shipped out vast numbers of cattle to Chicago and points east; plenty of railroaders swelled the crowds in the saloons and brothels.

Brilliant kerosene lanterns hung in the smoky air in all the saloons. Even in the middle of the street Slocum could hear the clink of bottles and the sound of chips being tossed onto the green baize tables. From the distance, near the river, came the sound of locomotives making up the cattle trains which would leave in the morning. Slocum stopped; the sound bothered him. He frowned, thinking hard. Someone bumped into him.

"Git outta my way, dude!" said a half-drunken cowboy.

Slocum turned and stared at the man. His face was hard and without expression. The cowboy realized he had made a mistake.

"No offense, mister," he stammered.

"None taken, sir," Slocum said, with the flat Northern accent he had been practicing. He watched the man clump away down the board sidewalk. He resumed his thinking. The locomotive sound—what did that remind him of? At last he remembered.

Months ago, when he had been very ill, lying in fever in the jacal, he had heard the war chants of the Apaches. There were chugging sounds from the drums and the shrill piercing blasts of the crane-wing whistles —very much like locomotives on the upgrade. A strangely exciting sound. He was pleased at first at having remembered, but then he thought of Idizhode and what she had done for him. He felt ashamed. And that made him think of Idagalele. He shook his head as if his thoughts could be dispelled by that act. They could not.

He strolled slowly along the board sidewalk. In a minute he had entered the Texas Star. It had received that name in order to appeal to the Texans who came north on their huge drives up to Colorado and Wyoming. It gave them everything cowboys wanted to see after months on the trail: huge paintings of naked women, a round mirror seven feet in diameter with a massive carved frame erupting in fat gilt cupids, a 40-foot-long mahogany bar and a brilliantly polished brass footrail, row on row of liquor in cut-glass decanters and a bowl of fresh lemons for the toddies.

In the rear there were ten tables covered with green baize, surrounded by comfortable chairs. It was a far cry from playing poker on a blanket with matches for chips, and the Texas Star always did a land-office business.

Slocum walked in and ordered a toddy. It was the kind of drink a gambler would order—there was a lot of water to dilute the whiskey, and it was a drink that could be sipped and stretched for over half an hour. Slocum intended to be always in control of his thinking and of his physical reflexes.

He leaned against the bar and surveyed the room. Near him was a table with six chairs. One was empty. The five men who were playing looked at him occasionally with curiosity. Slocum nodded pleasantly and continued to sip. He wanted to get in the game, but it was important not to seem overanxious.

Twenty minutes passed. One of the men turned around and said, "Evenin', stranger. Someone didn't show for the game. Care to join us?"

"Much obliged, sir," Slocum said. He sat down and bought a stack of dollar chips.

The men around the table were ranchers and businessmen of Socorro. The talk was of cattle. Slocum listened carefully. He could pick up information which could come in mighty handy some day, in case he should chance to pick up a few hundred head that might be lying around somewhere. Many buyers were not too particular as to ownership.

One hard-faced man of 50, with a hat that sat squarely on his head with a no-nonsense air and a heavy gold watch chain stretching tightly across his protruding belly, threw down his cards with disgust and yawned. "Thieves're destroyin' my cattle," he said. "Over to Santa Marta way they took about forty, Odell says."

"They ought to steal 'em all, goddamn you," snorted the tall man to Slocum's right. By the calm way the hard-faced man took the insult, Slocum knew they were good friends.

He went on. "That's the way you got yours."

"Prove it," the man said amiably.

"How, Ed? It happened too long ago. An' you know it."

"Yup," Ed grinned. He lit a cigar.

"You got a nice spread now, Ed."

"Yup. Big 'n' pretty, but hot damn, wouldn't it be fun to tear her up an' start all over again!" He drew on his cigar till he was satisfied. "Yuh know," he said, "I found out one thing, and I found it out just lately. I'm too old to break horses an' I ain't smart enough to teach school."

Slocum studied his cards. He had a ten for a hole card, and two tens were face up. The next card was a ten. He was concentrating on the other players' hands when he noticed they were all looking past him.

He heard a familiar voice say, "How come you didn' wait?"

It was Cameron.

Slocum could not control the sudden surge of hate that burst into his heart. It did not matter; his face was under absolute control. He took a long draw on his cigar.

"Shucks, man," said the hard-faced man, whose name was Morgan, "we waited half an hour. This gentleman looked like he wanted to play, so we invited him."

Slocum stood up and faced Cameron. They were two feet apart. This would be the acid test.

"Good evenin', sir," Slocum said calmly. "My name's Sheridan. Hope you've no objection. I'd be right happy to yield my seat."

"Nonsense," Morgan said sharply. "Can't see throwin' out a man whose money I'm lookin' to latch on to. Let's all jus' push our chairs a little closer. It's more friendly."

Morgan reached out and pulled an empty chair from the next table. Cameron sat down. After a moment Slocum sat. He let out his tension in a long slow exhalation. Cameron had stared at him and had not recognized him.

It had worked! The shaved mustache, the short, neatly trimmed hair instead of the mass flowing over his shirt, the gray in his hair, the pale, thin, clean-shaved face, the gambler's outfit instead of the worn, dirty range clothes Cameron had seen him in—it had worked!

A sudden wild joy swept over him. At first, when he had heard Cameron's voice the only thing he wanted to do was to jam his derringer into the man's stomach as far as his powerful shoulder muscles could drive it. After that he had imagined savoring the look on Cameron's face as the blood would drain out through fear, leaving it white and moist with sweat.

But now that he was unrecognized, Slocum decided with a shiver of pleasure that it would be far more pleasant to sit back and wait patiently for the correct moment of disclosure. If he had been as impulsive as he had at first been tempted to be, Cameron would have had only a few seconds in which to be terrified. It was not enough for Slocum. He had lost a lot of time through Cameron; two friends had been killed through his betrayal—and Slocum knew his shoulder would always ache in cold weather.

A few seconds for Cameron was not enough in exchange for all that. A few hours, better; a few days—marvelous!

"Raise you," Slocum said, and shoved more chips into the center of the table.

Morgan shoved out his chips. He suddenly chuckled. "Lookin' at all those chips reminds me," he said. "Had a game goin' on a train. Playin' with two cattle brokers from Chicago. An' a judge. An' a minister. Yep. A minister. The train goes into a tunnel an' they didn't light the lamps, an' when we come out into daylight, damned if each one of us wasn't sprawled flat over the table coverin' our chips with our arms an' whole bodies, too. You needn't look so insulted, Cameron. I call."

Slocum turned up his hole card.

"Can't beat that," Morgan said cheerfully. The others tossed in their cards.

"Been 'round here long?" Cameron asked.

"Just got in."

"Where you from?"

There was a sudden silence at the table. The dealer stopped shuffling the deck. It was very bad manners to ask questions like that, and Slocum could feel the tension tighten around him, as if someone were winding a clock spring.

"I'm from there," he said casually. He knew Cameron had not liked losing, and he had not liked the little joke Morgan had made about protecting the chips in the train in the tunnel.

" 'There'? Where's 'there'?" Cameron demanded. Slocum realized the man's speech was slurred. It was the kind of thing that could happen if you downed two or three quick drinks on an empty stomach. A few minutes would pass before one's tongue and movements would reveal the effects of that much alcohol on an empty stomach. And now Slocum remembered that this was the same kind of thing that Cameron used to do.

" 'There' is about seventy-three miles north of everywhere," he said.

The other men laughed, relieved that Slocum was not going to take offense. The dealer finished his shuffling with a relieved sigh.

"Cut," he said.

Cameron reached out and cut.

He was flushed and determined to show he was top man.

Morgan frowned. "You've just gone and formed yourself in a hollow square around a bottle of able-bodied whiskey, man," he said. "Maybe you ought to set this game out."

Cameron paid no attention. He wore his .45 low on his right hip, in the approved professional-gunman style, the way no working cowboy ever did. He had a habit of leaning forward and pretending to balance himself by spreading a palm on his thigh. This left his hand only four inches from the butt. Then he would leave the Colt in the holster, swivel it upwards and fire. It was very effective against anyone who did not know that this was his fighting style.

But Slocum knew all about it.

The cards were dealt out.

Cameron stared heavily at Slocum. He had formed an instant dislike to him. There was something about the man that made him uneasy. Cameron thought it was because of the neat grooming and his general dislike of people who played poker better than he could.

"Pick up your cards, man!" Morgan said crisply.

Cameron stretched out a left hand, tipped with his usually dirty fingernails. He pulled the cards towards him with one hand. The other hand remained in his lap.

Slocum was now watching him with dry amusement. His anger, which he feared would sweep him out of control, had dissipated. It would be too soon to kill Cameron. There would be no point in being forced into it now. Cameron would have to know who he was, and then think about it for a while; Slocum wanted the dirty, sweaty bastard to think about it at length before he died.

Cameron awkwardly raked the cards together. He squared them off. Slocum watched the other men at the table. They were annoyed. Then Cameron fanned them out, stared at them and put them down in an awed manner. He had completely forgotten his quarrel with Slocum.

Slocum looked at his cards. Three kings, one jack, one four. He discarded the jack and the four and picked the fourth king and a ten.

Cameron stood pat. His face was flushed. His other hand had come up from its ready position on his right thigh. He was never able to play poker impassively, Slocum remembered. Slocum knew the man had something excellent.

Cameron's stubby, filthy fingers kept squaring and resquaring his cards. The spectacle of this natural slob neatly aligning his cards amused Slocum even more. He made no attempt to hide his feelings.

Cameron glared at him venomously and triumphantly. He was absolutely convinced that he was about to show himself the better player of the two men. Slocum raised him twice, just to get the man excited. Then he calmly spoke.

"I pass," he said.

Cameron's face fell. He displayed a royal flush, his hands trembling in excitement. When he turned triumphantly towards Slocum, he found the gambler politely smothering a yawn. *A royal flush,* Cameron thought angrily, the best in my whole life, and this goddamn dude is tryin' to pretend it ain't nothin'! Probably the first and last time anybody here has seen one and this sucker has to yawn and sneer.

A hate arose deep within Cameron. He made the resolve right then that he would settle the man's hash some day.

Slocum's quick amusement had disappeared. He realized that Cameron had quite probably bought his chips with the money he had gotten from the sheriff for his betrayal. He stared back at Cameron with a tight little smile.

"Well, gentlemen," he said, standing up, "I started out this mornin' pretty early. If you'll excuse me, I think I'll get a little sleep. If you've no objections, I'd be pleased if we could resume playin' tomorrow."

"No objections 'tall," Morgan said. The other men nodded their agreement.

Slocum bowed slightly and left. After a moment Cameron staggered to his feet, lurched to the bar and ordered a drink.

Watching him, Morgan said "I bet the two of 'em 'll be swappin' lead in a week or so. Any takers?"

There were no takers.

11

The next day was Sunday. And Sunday was the day when the sheriff and his brand-new wife went to church.

When they walked in Slocum had been in his pew at the right rear for 15 minutes. He sat calmly, with his hat on his lap as if he had been going to church every Sunday in his life. But he had not entered one for 15 years.

Then Hamilton came in with his wife on his arm.

"Ain't she jus' the purtiest thing?" sighed a woman in front of Slocum.

"Nope, second," retorted her husband. "Purtiest thing is a herd of red Herefords in a spring pasture, but she's second, you bet."

Mrs. Hamilton was a redheaded woman and she wore a green silk dress. Her hair was piled atop her narrow head, exposing her tiny ears. She did not wear a corset and did not need one. She twirled a small white lace parasol, and as she paused in the aisle, very well aware that people were talking about her, she took out a small white handkerchief from her handbag, ferreted out some hairpins and pinned the handkerchief to her hair.

Hamilton stood beside her, flushing with pride. He held her parasol in one thick red hand and clutched the stub of an expensive Havana in the other. He stood surveying the congregation. Slocum thought he was collecting the admiring glances as if he meant to paste them in a scrapbook.

Mrs. Hamilton made quite a production out of the handkerchief. She knew that her uplifted arms were making her breasts quiver under the tight green silk, and Slocum, watching her, felt himself beginning to dislike her smug arrogance.

"She's so terrible stuck-up," whispered the woman in front of Slocum.

"Yup, but I'm gettin' up a powerful head of steam jus' lookin'," replied her husband. Slocum smiled. The couple had neatly expressed his conflicting feelings. Part of him thoroughly disliked her calm assumption of superiority over everyone in this raw frontier town; the other part wanted to tear off that green silk dress and make her beg to be made love to.

Finished with her primping, Mrs. Hamilton then moved sinuously up the aisle, her hips packed tightly into her dress. She sat down. With a proud look around, Hamilton subsided his heavy bulk next to her. All through the services Slocum stared at the tiny handkerchief surrounded by the burnished red copper of her hair. He had never seen hair quite that color, and he suddenly had a picture of what her naked body would look like, under some cottonwoods. There the hot sunlight, filtering down through the leafy canopy, would create a pale green light which would filter back and forth over her unpinned red hair and the carroty red tangle of hair at her groin . . . He was glad when the services were over.

Slocum stood up and moved outside, to the sun-baked grass. He lit a cigar and waited. The Hamiltons emerged; he deliberately positioned himself so that Hamilton would have to notice him. To make doubly sure, he removed his cigar and bowed slightly as soon as Mrs. Hamilton happened to glance in his direction.

She nodded politely. Hamilton nodded also. Slocum was watching Hamilton's face intently, and he was sure that there was no sign of recognition at all. Then the Hamiltons were caught up in a group of townspeople. They were laughing and chatting. Slocum replaced his hat and put the cigar in his mouth again, looking at Mrs. Hamilton. He knew she would ultimately turn in his direction. When she did so, within ten seconds, pretending she wanted to talk to someone, he lifted his hat and bowed even more deeply than before.

The thought of pulling off that Hamilton bitch's underdrawers—with her husband suspecting it was going to happen—and being powerless to do anything about it—oh, that delighted Slocum. He couldn't lock her up every time he had to leave Socorro on business. And he would *have* to leave Socorro frequently—he was the sheriff.

The whole thing delighted Slocum.

What was that line from an old book out of which his father used to read aloud to him when he was a child? What was it? It was, yes, *now* he had it: "Revenge is a dish best eaten cold."

Slocum shoved his hands in his pockets and went off whistling down the street. He overtook the couple who had been sitting in front of him. As he passed he heard her whisper to her husband, "That feller ought to be ashamed, whistlin' on the Lord's Day!"

12

On Monday Slocum rented a light buggy at Reilly's Livery Stable and drove slowly along the street that went past the sheriff's house. It was a substantial white frame dwelling, boasting a veranda above which flowed the elaborate arabesques of carpenter gothic. A white picket fence ran around a sunbaked yard where patches of grass grimly tried to grow under the pitiless sun. A few shrubs leaned in a dispirited fashion against the veranda, but the deficiencies of the landscaping were redeemed by the view to the west. There a huge ominous purple mass of the mountains hung under the brilliant turquoise sky.

She was not in sight. He drove out a few miles, past adobe houses with their festoons of red chiles drying in the sun and goats tied to shrubs or to fences made of planted cactus. The road forked. The right branch went towards the mountains, the left branch curved towards the river. He turned left. After a while it ran past cornfields, then alongside an icy little creek that bounced and tumbled down from the remote mountains before it slowed down on the flats and meandered, lined with cottonwoods, to its confluence with the Rio Grande.

Little clusters of adobe houses were everywhere along the creek. Corn, melons and tomatoes were lush. They grew thickly with the heat and the water for irrigation.

He had seen enough. He turned around and drove back. At the sheriff's house he was sure he saw the upstairs curtains drawn back as he passed. He lifted his hat and bowed. The curtains flashed back into place. Two women gossiping across the road were staring at him. They had seen everything, he was sure. Good, good.

He returned the buggy. Cameron was in the yard pitching horeshoes with a hostler. When he saw Slocum he spun his horseshoe with a vicious, angry twist without looking at the iron pipe sunk into the ground. The shoe ringed it perfectly.

Slocum nodded pleasantly.

"Good shot," he said.

"Let's see *you* do it," Cameron said heavily, his voice tense with challenge.

"No, thanks. My game's poker."

"Playin' tonight?"

"Yes."

"Same saloon?"

Slocum nodded.

"How 'bout you an' me?"

"It would be a pleasure, sir."

Somewhere Cameron had acquired a beautiful .45. Its handle was like a deck of cards: all the suits had been cut out of silver and inlaid in the butt. He had rolled up his gun belt and placed it carefully on a bench next to the stable while he was pitching horseshoes. He picked up the belt and buckled. He noticed Slocum glancing at it.

"Nice, huh?" he demanded.

Slocum gave it his sincere admiration.

"Feel the balance," Cameron demanded.

Slocum hefted it.

"Damn fine gun," he said, and handed it back.

"Bought it in a hock shop in Albuquerque," Cameron boasted. "Cost me three hundred bucks. Goddamn that's a beautiful gun!"

Yes, Slocum said silently, and I know how you got the money, you dirty bastard. He felt the old rage rising within, the old uncontrollable rage which used to swell up and explode like a huge ocean wave, in which he was powerless to do anything but allow himself to be swept along in its naked, blind power.

It would be easy to grab the gun and pistol-whip Cameron about the head, and then shoot him as he was on his knees. The thought was very tempting; what held him back was the knowledge that this foolishness would remove Hamilton and his redheaded, arrogant wife from his grasp. It would not be smart, he told himself. He had to check himself.

He thrust his hands deep into his pockets, as if by imprisoning them in this manner they would be unable to grab Cameron's Colt. He was so close he could smell the man's stale sweat. Cameron turned and walked away with his usual tuneless whistling. Months ago, while they were still partners, Slocum had thanked God that the both of them had never passed a winter in line camp. He would have killed the man by spring just because of that piercing, off-key shrilling.

Slocum stood there motionless, watching Cameron walk away.

There was only one way to handle the situation, Slocum felt. He would have to call a sharp halt to any argument which might develop with the man. Even if it meant backing down.

Even if it meant he would look like a coward.

13

"Gimme four cards," Cameron said with disgust.

Slocum tossed him four cards. He took two. Morgan took two. Only the three of them were playing. It was Monday night and the saloon was almost empty.

Cameron had been losing all night. From time to time he rubbed his gun butt with his right palm. He imagined that this kept the silver insets polished—and that it, as well, gave him good luck. Morgan was amused by this. The old rancher wore his gun on the left hip, butt forward. He liked the cross draw. Slocum was sitting to the right of Morgan.

Cameron's cards were bad. He compounded his bad luck by playing stupidly. He had been drinking steadily. At midnight Morgan sent for sandwiches, but Cameron refused to eat.

The coffee was the same color and worse-tasting than the river flowing a hundred yards away, but Slocum had learned not to be particular. He picked up a can of condensed milk and poured some in. Morgan said, "Somethin' I never been able to figger out. They's eight thousand cows within a couple miles o' here, an' we send to Chicago for milk in a can. Don't make sense."

"I'll tell yuh why," Cameron said. He stood up and swayed as he recited:

"Here's to Carnation Milk,
The finest in the land.
No tits to pull,
No hay to pitch,
Just punch a hole
In the son of a bitch!"

Slocum did not laugh.

"You don't like that poem?" Cameron demanded.

"Who wants to know?"

"Why, I do, goddamnit!" His speech was slurred with alcohol.

"Well," Slocum said calmly, "how do you like the way you found out?"

Morgan roared with laughter. He dealt.

Cameron's pile of chips was very low. He bet them all even though Slocum had asked for just one card. Slocum had two sixes showing; Cameron's highest card on view was a ten. Slocum turned up his hole card and displayed three sixes. Cameron's hole card was a ten. Slocum looked at him in contempt and raked in the pot.

Cameron's mouth opened and hung loose. He drew up a big gob of phlegm with a long, rattling, nauseating hawk, and Slocum was sure that the man intended to spray him with the mouthful of mucus.

God give me patience! Slocum said to himself, and decided to crawl if, in fact, Cameron would spray him. The best way to handle it would be to laugh it off, and excuse it as the mindless act of a drunk. He could get away with that for an explanation.

But Cameron suddenly turned his head aside and delivered the spittle into a spittoon. Slocum let out a long, slow exhalation, and watched as Cameron, his uncombed hair shaggy as a buffalo's, swung his head back and stared at Slocum.

Cameron was drunk. Or he would not have done what he now did, which was to suddenly draw his Colt, without any sentence of explanation for his motive. It was a very dangerous thing to do, and especially so in front of John Slocum. His intention was to see if Slocum would want to buy it. That would give him a couple of hundred dollars to buy enough chips to stay in the game. But the man was too drunk to realize that he should have stated his intentions before reaching for the butt.

Slocum was not wearing a gun. In his right pocket he had his small, two-barreled derringer, but he knew he couldn't reach it in time. But next to him was Morgan, with his Colt on his left, butt facing forward. Slocum twisted to his left, put his left palm on the old man's chest, reached across him, and grabbed the gun butt. As he pulled out the Colt with his right hand, he pushed Morgan's chest hard with his left. The startled rancher went over backwards, and in the cleared area where Morgan's chair had been standing Slocum dove flat and came up under the table on his knees.

His left hand was braced to keep him upright, and his right hand shot out to its full length. The barrel sank three inches into Cameron's stomach.

"Don't make a move, you sonofabitch. Or I'll unload this in your guts. Put that gun back in. Real slow, now."

Morgan, still on his back on the floor, thought that the words sounded like a series of icicles snapping off one by one. Later he told a friend that Slocum's voice sounded like a frosted crowbar.

Cameron's gun had been withdrawn three inches from its holster. Drunk as he was, he froze, his mouth open in astonishment. He slid the gun back in very slowly, following orders. Then he raised his hands and bent over to peer under the table.

"Now why the hell didja do *that?*" he demanded in honest amazement. "I wanted to sell my gun is all, damnit!"

Slocum realized the man was telling the truth. He got to his feet, helped Morgan up, set their chairs in place again, dusted Morgan off and begged everyone's pardon.

Of course it was Cameron's fault. Morgan rasped: "Man, don't you know better than to whip out your gun in a card game without 'splainin' why? That's plain fool stupid."

Everyone was quiet for a long awkward minute. Finally Slocum broke the embarrassed silence and asked Cameron how much he wanted for the gun.

"I paid three hunnerd in Albuquerque," Cameron repeated.

It was possibly true. Without saying a word, Slocum pushed three hundred dollars' worth of chips across the table. Cameron shoved his Colt across the table. Slocum thrust it inside his belt. Morgan cleared his throat and spoke for the first time since the beginning of the incident.

"It's sixty years since I first took a center shot at daylight," he said, "and mister, I ain't never seen *anythin'* like that. Never saw a gambler move like you. You came down on him like the whole Missouri on a sandbar. I didn't even have an umbrella to hide behind. I was awful nervous, folks."

"Your turn to deal, sir," Slocum said. He didn't like Morgan's remarks. They might encourage Cameron to smell him out some more; to backtrack and check out his record as a gambler. If he would go and do it, the trail would peter out pretty fast. And a man like Samuel Sheridan didn't just appear in Silver City out of nowhere. How come he hadn't left any traces anywhere else? Slocum hoped that Cameron wouldn't have the time or energy.

"All's well that ends well," Slocum said placidly. "Gimme two cards, Mr. Morgan."

On his way back to the hotel, three hours later, Slocum heard footsteps coming up rapidly behind him on the board sidewalk. He pulled the Colt and turned. Cameron was close behind him. In spite of his bulk, Cameron, like many big men, could move fast. Slocum's hand gripped the gun butt.

"Mr. Sheridan." Cameron's voice was thick with whiskey.

"Yes."

"Like to talk to you."

"Go ahead."

"It's private. Got a deal you might like."

"Well?"

"Well——" Cameron, still drunk, lurched unsteadily against a hitching rack and held on for support. "Make good money. You wanna hear, meetcha at Reilly's tomorrow. 'Bout nine. All right?"

Slocum was curious.

"All right," he said. "Nine."

"Like the way you play poker. Smart."
"Yes."
"You deserve 'at gun. Gambler's gun. An' you won it gamblin'. Fittin'! Nine, you hear?"

He pushed himself away from the hitching rack and lurched away. Slocum watched him. Did the man want him to walk into an ambush? Not likely, in such a public place, and at a time when the streets would be full of people. Slocum looked forward to their meeting.

14

When Slocum walked up to Reilly's Livery next morning Cameron was sitting in a hitched-up buggy.

"Hoss is et," he said curtly. "Hop in." He obviously had a splitting headache.

Slocum didn't move. Had the man found out who he was? Was he going to be taken directly into an ambush in a nicely chosen isolated spot, there to be dry-gulched without ceremony?

"C'mon, c'mon," said Cameron, impatiently patting the black leather seat beside him.

He swung up and sat down. The man's smell came off him as if he were an uncurried horse himself. Slocum forced himself to make no sign of irritation as he sat as close to Cameron as he could without making him suspicious. He wanted to force any sniper—if there should be one—to hesitate lest he shoot Cameron too. Cameron said nothing as they trotted through town. When they were well on the road towards the mountains, he spoke.

"Mr. Sheridan, you please lissen. Admit I kinda disliked you at first—an' I still do. But when you thought I was draggin' my Colt, I thought I never saw nothin' so fast—like the way you come into action.

The way you knocked ole Morgan over to git him outta the way in case I fired, the way you grabbed his gun same time an' rolled over on your stummick an' covered me! Hombre, that was quick thinkin'! So I got to thinkin' some more. I c'n use you."

"How?"

"Depends on whether you're willin' to risk some gunplay."

"Depends on how much."

So the goddamn fool was roping him into something! Oh, Slocum thought, suppressing a smile, wouldn't it be great if he found out enough to betray Cameron to someone like a U.S. marshal! For money, of course.

"So you're innarested?"

"Sure."

Cameron grinned. "All right. You jus' wait a while."

It didn't smell like any dry-gulching situation. Slocum relaxed a little. But he kept his hands in his coat pockets. The fingers of his right hand were curled around the derringer butt. The horses trotted easily. It was a sharp, cool morning, and they were climbing a long, easy grade. Far behind them, and far below, in a jumbled maze of white adobe blocks, Socorro sat, with green splotches here and there. Then came the double silver thread of the railroad running north to Albuquerque and south to Las Cruces. Then came the wide, calm brown snake of the Rio Grande, with its crescent-shaped sandbars on which lay scattered sun-bleached tree trunks deposited there by the spring floods.

A few miles farther, halfway down a sharp descent, Cameron pulled the buggy over onto a level stretch. Far to their right lay Socorro and the river, to their left was the desert and even farther to the left was the black, savage loom of the mountains.

"Good view, huh?"

Slocum nodded. High in the piercing blue sky floated a vulture. Out of curiosity he had been clocking it mentally. It soared without a wing flap for seven minutes.

"Been out there?"

Slocum nodded again.

"Me too," Cameron said, with a burst of feeling that surprised Slocum a little. "Every goddamn bush is full of thorns. No water. You dry up, you walk around creakin'. You touch anythin', it stings. You pet it, it bites. You eat, it kills you. An' in a couple weeks it'll be midsummer, they got the most beautiful specimens of rattlesnakes out there, all scattered around everywhere, like whores on payday. Jesus Christ Almighty!"

Cameron's obvious fear of rattlers amused Slocum. He had no fear of them. He treated them carefully and gave their favorite areas wide berth. Unlike many cowboys he never shot one just for target practice. He appreciated their warning rattles, and when he heard one, he gave way. Compared to Cameron, for instance, they were the soul of honor.

Cameron suddenly brightened. "Look down there —see that dust?"

Far below, outside Socorro, he pointed to a tiny brown puffball. It seemed to be tied to a small black beetle.

"That's Mrs. Hamilton's black sulky. She likes to ride 'round in it. Rides up to Zia Pueblo. Buys Navajo blankets and them jars from Acoma. Sticks 'em all over the house. Goes by herself, too. You know what I'd like to do to that stuck-up woman?"

Slocum knew. He wanted to do it himself. He listened patiently as Cameron went on with his list. He added angrily, "I do plenty for the sheriff. I say 'good mornin', ma'am,' she don't even look at me. She treats me like some kind a animal!" He brooded in angry silence for a while. Slocum sat and listened. He had learned long ago the best way to find out things was to keep his mouth shut and be patient.

"Now, looka here, you see them mountains? Back inside 'em, mebbe thirty, thirty-five miles, is the Dirty Dog Mine. You ever hear of it?"

Slocum had heard of it. It was the Dirty Dog's shipment of bullion that he had tried for with Cameron and Wells and Bond only three months ago. It seemed another lifetime ago.

"Nope," Slocum said.

"They take gold outta the quartz ore, they got a big stampin' mill. Goes on day an' night. Shakes the whole town. They melt it down into bars. Ever' two, three weeks they ship it down in a stagecoach. With two guards. Some of it rides in the boot, more inside, like it was passengers. It comes to meet the train. But nobody knows what day they ship, see? Ain't it better to take the gold offa two men up here where nobody c'n see, than to try to take it offa train where they c'n shoot out the winders an' Lord knows how many more men they got hidden? Eh?"

"Makes a lot of sense," Slocum said, judiciously.

Damn right, he said to himself. You damn fool, if you would have thought of that, you'd be a damn sight better off right now. But maybe not—not with Cameron along to work out some kind of a stab in the back.

"See why I brung you here? It's our chance to sit in the shade an' smoke big long black seegars the rest of our lives. We're gonna be rich. I mean *rich*. An' I know what to do with it. Not like that broken-down ole sonofabitch Morgan who thinks he's better'n me. He's got a li'l bitty spread outside o' town, a couple thousand acres is all, an' thinks he's God Almighty.

He's been follerin' cows so long all he knows is stand in the middle of the street an' paw an' beller. Hell, I ain't gonna wind up like *that*."

Slocum lit a cigar. Ever since he had come back he had deliberately forced himself to acquire different habits.

He had always rolled his own cigarettes. Since he had come into Silver City he smoked nothing but cigars. It was attention to such small details that had made him so successful. Until he met Cameron. And now it looked like Cameron himself was going to even the score.

"Now," said Cameron, "right here the road gets so steep them six horses pullin' the stage are movin' at a walk. If we jus' move back a bit, right here where we're sittin', we c'n still see 'em, an' they can't see us."

Cameron jumped out of the buggy. "Like we stand here," he said. "See? We c'n see far down the road. An' they can't see us."

"Right."

"We step out. They can't get the horses goin' any faster. They got no room to turn around. We get the drop. They move, they're dead. They know it. So they stop, right? We cut the horses loose. We take 'em with us. We take their boots. They got a seven-, eight-hour walk to town!" He grinned triumphantly.

Not bad, Slocum thought. It needed refinement, like gold quartz. But it was very good.

"How do you know what day they'll come?"

"I hang 'round the sheriff's office. I keep my ears open. They have to tell the sheriff so's he c'n arrange an escort while they wait for the train."

Slocum mused.

"How do we split?" he asked.

"Seventy-thirty."

What a cheap bastard, Slocum thought. When he had taken Cameron in, the deal was, as always with

Slocum, ten percent off the top for him for his planning and his expenses—everything else was shared equally.

"No deal."

"I thought of it. I got the information."

Slocum used to think of jobs too. He'd be damned if he'd change his principles.

"No."

"All right. Sixty-forty."

"Half."

"No. No!"

"Let's go back. I've enjoyed the ride."

"It's gotta be sixty-forty."

"You can always find someone else at that figure. Not me."

Cameron spat and chewed his lower lip. He looked at the desert. He looked at the mountains. He looked briefly and venomously at Slocum. Birds were singing in the clear air. The mountains looked as if the two men could walk there in ten minutes. They were 40 miles away.

"All right," Cameron said, in a sullen, slow growl.

"Half and half?"

"Yeah."

"What about expenses?"

"What expenses?"

Slocum stared. The man was serious.

He sighed. "You expect to hang around Socorro afterwards?"

"Sure," Cameron said, with some indignation. "For a while. I don't want 'em to figger out I done it, right? I'm hidin' my share. An' when it cools off, I light out for Mexico." He clapped his hands together and shot out his right hand south, like an arrow in flight. The horse jerked up his head when he heard the report of the two palms slapping. The wind came blowing up the hill, bringing the scent of the pines over which it had lazily drifted on its way down from the mountains. Slocum waited patiently a few seconds. When it became clear that Cameron had finished, Slocum said, "And that's it?"

Cameron nodded, pleased with his own cleverness.

Slocum tilted his hat over his forehead, crossed his arms and slid down deep into his seat. The wind changed direction. Now it blew cool against his face, bringing with it the scent of the sagebrush crushed by the buggy's wheels. He kept his voice calm, struggling to conceal the contempt he felt.

"We've got to have new horses. Horses they've never seen 'round Socorro. We can't go an' rent 'em from Reilly's Livery. So they'll think we're strangers. We've got to wear clothes we never wore in Socorro—and never will wear again. So we've got to have an extra set of clothes. An' boots. We need shotguns. You got a shotgun?"

Cameron shook his head with a slow, sullen shake. Slocum had seen that particular kind of head movement before—it had come from a grizzly he had come upon unexpectedly. It was an old boar, with a festering, broken-off arrow in one shoulder, and it had immediately charged. Slocum got off a snap shot with his Winchester, too low. The boar halted for a second, disconcerted by the sudden pain in his chest, and had then shaken his head for four or five seconds, and had then resumed the charge.

"No shotgun? I don't have one either. The guards might take a chance an' draw against our Winchesters, but they'll think twice 'bout a double-barreled shotgun filled with lead slugs in each barrel pointin' straight at their guts. Then we're gonna need a few good burros."

"Burros?"

"How much you think gold weighs, for crissake?" Slocum demanded. He was beginning to lose patience.

"Yeah, it's heavy," Cameron mumbled.

"How much gold will they carry?"

"Two million dollars' worth, that's what they carry."

"Let's see," said Slocum. "Gold at thirty dollars an ounce. Five hundred a pound. And five hundred dollars into two million is . . . four thousand pounds. Two tons! Two tons of gold, man. A good, strong burro carries four hundred pounds. And four hundred pounds into four thousand pounds goes ten times. Ten burros!"

"Never thought of that."

"Think about it. Or what you plannin' on? Buryin' the gold right here so you won't need burros?"

His voice was thick with contempt. Cameron flushed with anger. Slocum relented. He didn't want to push the man too far right then.

"Suppose you bury it right here. How?"

"Jus' dig."

"How, man? There's 'bout four inches of dirt. Then comes lava. Lava! Solid rock. How the hell you gonna bury two *tons?* An' supposin' you work a miracle and you bury it here—how you gonna make it look as if the ground wasn't ever disturbed when they come back with a posse to pick up the trail?"

"So what'll we do?" Cameron asked. His anger had disappeared. In its place was a childish plaintiveness.

"The lava runs like this for miles. We take an extra burro along. He'll carry picks, shovels, extra water bags, oats. The lava comes up to the surface down there. We won't leave any tracks on the lava. The posse'll think we buried it somewhere 'round here. They'll go over every square foot around here for miles lookin'. Or they'll think we picked it up in a buckboard and maybe headed back to town. So they'll go lookin' all over Socorro for the buckboard. They'll go into every barn between here an' the river. That'll all take a lot of time. An' in the meantime we'll be hittin' Clear Creek on the other side of the lava beds. Lots of trees along the creek. Ground underneath is soft. It's just twenty miles south of the road from Albuquerque to Fort Wingate.

"We dig a hole and bury it. 'Bout three miles west is a deep barranca. We kill the horses an' drop 'em in. We ditch the clothes we wore an' the shotguns. We get rid of 'em."

"*Dump* good shotguns?"

"Yep. We dump 'em. Because what the hell are two prospectors doin' with shotguns? Don't make sense. We kill most of the burros. Then we ride into Fort Wingate or Gallup or even into Prescott. We say we're prospectors and we say our luck has played out, an' we're sick of the whole damn business, we're goin' back to cowboyin'. We sell our outfit for what we c'n get for it. We take the train to Albuquerque. An' then we separate an' we come back to Socorro a week apart."

Cameron looked at him with his dogged, heavy, sullen face. It was hard with suspicion.

Slocum was prepared. He had come to rely upon his radically changed appearance. In fact, when he had first looked into the barbershop mirror in Silver City, and had seen himself without his heavy black mustache, he had been startled. He actually had not recognized himself in the thin, high-cheekboned image that stared back at him. The pain of his wound and his grim determination to get even had etched deep lines around his mouth. He was startled at the amount of gray hairs. He lit another cigar, a mannerism he knew Cameron would never connect with the Slocum who had waited with him for the train to come chugging south from Socorro.

"Don't like the plan?" Slocum asked.

"Sure I like it. It's real smart."

"But you don't like part of it?"

Slocum knew what part Cameron didn't like. But he wanted the man to say it aloud himself. He enjoyed the ponderous working of Cameron's mind. It was as transparent to him as the gears moving in a glass-enclosed clock. For a second the thought came to him that Cameron had been smart enough to betray him once: Was he planning a clever scheme to ensnare him? He decided to make a little test.

He had done that test before with other people, very intelligent people—and it had frequently worked. It was very simple: Slocum talked, never looking at the other man's face. He would seemingly let himself be persuaded by what the other man was saying, especially if he were sure that the man was lying. More and more he would give the impression he was being drawn into the plan, or being convinced.

And very suddenly he would look sharply into the man's face.

Frequently he had surprised a look of contempt or hatred. And if not on the face, it would be in the eyes. Only the rarest of people could keep their real emotions out of their eyes. If their eyes and face remained placid and clear, then it was safe to trust the man.

"All right," Slocum said. "I know what you're thinkin'. So we'll take five mules apiece when we get to Clear Creek. We'll split. You go where you want, I go where I want. We'll each bury our gold no one knows where. An' then each of us will go back whenever he wants an' take what he wants."

Only relief showed in Cameron's face. If he wanted to kill Slocum and take his gold, it would be an idea that would come later. But right now he needed Slocum to organize and run things. There would be time to worry later, Slocum thought, but not till they came to Clear Creek.

But it was time now to give the donkey something to sweat about.

"But where's the money?" Slocum asked.

"The money?"

Oh, my God, Slocum thought, he knows as much about planning these things as a hog knows about Sundays.

"For the burros," Slocum said patiently. "For the shotguns. For the horses. For the picks an' shovels. For the clothes an' boots we'll use an' throw away. For supplies. For livin' in Fort Wingate. For the train —Jesus, man, did you think we'd *sell* some bullion along the way?"

"Oh. Yeah. Sure, you're right, Sheridan."

Yes. I'm right, Slocum thought. I'm wrong frequently. I blow things. I make mistakes. I trust the wrong people, like this animal I'm sitting next to. He's cunning once in a while. I *know* that. But I'm not so smart. I get tired sometimes. Make an early camp when I'm tired when I know I should ride. That's how come I spent two years in Montana Territorial Prison. But I don't make the same mistake twice. Not much consolation. Better not to make the mistake the first time.

"But I ain't got no money," Cameron was saying.

"Sure you do."

"But I tell yuh I ain't."

Slocum looked at him, taking a long deep draw on his cigar.

"I hear you collect from the tables around town, Cameron."

"I collect plenty, sure. I ain't hidin' nothin'. But it sure don't stay in *my* pocket."

"Where does it go?"

"To the vigilantes."

"An' that's the sheriff?"

"Yeah, he set it up. I jus' go 'round collectin'. I hand it over to Dawson."

"Dawson?"

"He looks like his jaw was busted in three places an' it all healed on one side. 'At's because it *is* busted in three places. I done it."

Slocum had seen Dawson, a surly, quiet drunk who always drank alone at the end of the bar.

"I broke it with a two-by-four 'cause he held out fifteen bucks on me."

"Loan?"

"Nope. We pulled a little robbery down in Las Cruces once when we was broke. I held the guy and Dawson went through his pockets. Later he gimme twenty bucks, that's half, an' then he drank hisself unconscious. I went through his pockets an' he had stuck fifteen bucks in his boots. I jus' picked up a two-by-four I found in the alley right next to him, and I jus' gave him a good whop on the face. He never knew it was me what done it." Cameron chuckled at the memory. He resumed. "Dawson gives it to Hamilton. An' Hamilton goes an' buys a pianner for the wife. He takes more of that money, the grafting sonofabitch, an' he buys her a Kentucky roan for her goddamn sulky. The horse cost eleven hundred dollars! Now I hear she wants a pack of greyhounds. I'm supposed to raise the money for that stuck-up whore."

"Can't you hold some out?"

"Nothin' wrong with the sheriff's arithmetic."

"Why don't you quit?"

Suddenly Cameron didn't want to talk about it anymore.

Slocum knew why. All Hamilton had to do to keep Cameron in line was to threaten to expose him for a stool pigeon. Some gunman would then kill him on general principles. Slocum changed the subject.

"You expect me to pay out maybe a thousand bucks? For *fifty* percent? And plan it, too? Because you ain't planned *anythin'*. You just brought your savvy of the time the bullion's comin' down from the Dirty Dog. 'At's important, sure. But you're just a finger man, up to now. You know what a finger man gets?"

Cameron said nothing.

"Well, how much?"

Finally Cameron spoke. "Ten percent," he growled. He gouged the words out of his throat reluctantly.

"Right. If we put up five hundred each for expenses, *then* we split fifty-fifty. I'd throw the plannin' in for nothin' extra. But if I put up the thousand all by myself, I *got* to have a bigger split."

Slocum savored the anguish on Cameron's face.

His voice choking with rage, Cameron said incredulously, "But there's gonna be a *million* for you. A million! An' you still——"

"Fifty-five–forty-five."

"Now look here!" Cameron's face was reddening.

"Sixty-forty is better."

"Goddamn it to hell! It's my idea, goddamn it!"

"Seventy-thirty."

"Why, you——" But Cameron caught himself. He subsided.

"You c'n swear till the sky turns yeller. Lissen to me. Anyone c'n get an idea. You got that one. Good. It's a good idea. Now, make it *work*. You already made plenty of mistakes, an' I proved it to you. Didn't I?" Cameron said nothing. Slocum had come to like the way he could make Cameron growl his reluctant assents, and so he repeated, "Didn't I?"

He waited, looking patiently at Cameron.

Cameron would not look at Slocum. He looked down at the stubby humps marking the approach to the desert, little hills which looked like they had been hammered back when they tried to get up. It was hotter now below, and already the desert floor was quivering with the heat waves. All of its morning color had flattened out. It was just brown.

"Yeah," Cameron finally muttered.

"I don' make mistakes. I see 'em before they happen. So they don't happen. You would've had the bullion an' no way to carry it. No way to bury it! An' you'd be wearin' your own clothes, an' ridin' your own horse, an' with people on the stagecoach who you'd be seein' in Socorro the same night! I want seventy-thirty. I'm worth it. Take it or leave it."

Cameron took it. What pleased Slocum enormously was that he had reversed the percentage deal. And 70 percent of $2,000,000 was $1,400,000.

He could buy a very good ranch with that. In Mexico, where they had never heard of extradition. He would fence it into pastures, buy good bulls, and stop running. Breed up fine beef cattle, keep the bloodlines clean. And never deal with people like Cameron anymore.

And this scum beside him would be responsible for that ranch.

He turned and looked at Cameron. The man was biting his lip and thinking hard. He didn't like the new percentage at all.

Very well, Slocum thought. He could change that. One hundred percent of $2,000,000 was $2,000,000. The question was who would do it first.

15

Slocum didn't have the thousand dollars. He began to gamble carefully. His luck was good; he put the money together in five nights. Gambling was hard work. He slept during the day. He woke up early, rented a horse at Reilly's and rode down to the river. He swam for the exercise. The swimming was good for his shoulder. He would have to be in very good condition for that desert ride he and Cameron were planning. He had seen men break down physically under hard living conditions—men who had eaten foolishly and who had drunk too much. It was not going to happen to him.

On these rides he took along the Colt he had bought from Cameron and practiced shooting at moving objects. He threw pieces of wood into the river. He would holster the Colt, throw a bottle high into the air and explode it in the air.

When he had been with the Apaches he had seen how they trained their young boys to be warriors. Each day they were dropped into the river. In winter, Nachodise told him, the father chopped a hole into the ice for the daily swim. Each day the boy would pull up a small bush. As the boy grew older he would move on to larger and larger bushes. Of course, the time would come when he wouldn't be able to budge the tree he was wrestling out of the earth, but the effort developed powerful back and shoulder muscles. In the summer the band moved down to the desert. A young boy would take a mouthful of water. His father would point to a peak ten miles away, and the boy would race off and run back. At the end of his 20-mile run across the desert, with the sun overhead, when all the desert animals lay panting in whatever shade they could find, the boy would run up to his father and spit out the mouthful of water to prove he hadn't swallowed it. By the time an Apache boy reached 14, Slocum knew he could easily beat the average cavalryman in physical combat.

Slocum admired the training. So, every morning, before he swam, he rode out to the desert, where no one could see what he was doing, and he would run up and down the brush-covered slopes, scaring the hell out of brilliant little green lizards and an occasional desert fox which lay panting under a cholla.

Once, riding back from the desert, he saw Mrs. Hamilton coming towards him in her black sulky. He stopped and slowly lifted his hat, deliberately maneuvering his horse till it halted broadside on to the sulky. She could either go around him, and into the ditch, or stop. She stopped, and frostily inclined her head an inch. She was wearing the white lace dress that Ching Yee said he hated to iron.

"Good mornin', ma'am," Slocum said politely.

"Good morning, Mr. Sheridan. I see you have no manners."

"On the contrary, ma'am. You're not wearin' a hat. This sun is almighty deceivin'. Easterners don't realize that till they turn all white an' sweaty, an' faint. I stopped you to tell you all 'bout it."

"I find it very pleasant and cool, Mr. Sheridan. And I see you have no manners."

Slocum grinned. "Ma'am. You're the only breath of cool air in the valley. I see you've been interested enough to ask people for my name."

She nodded calmly. "I'm always curious when I find anyone with such bad manners. If you please." She turned her horse's head in order to bypass him. Slocum backed up his horse two feet and blocked her again.

"Be good enough to get out of the way, please."

Her face was turning pink.

"Soon, soon. I see our good sheriff is insistin' you wear a corset."

She flushed. That was two things he had said which were simply never mentioned to respectable women. He had used the word "sweaty." And he had mentioned her corset. Slocum had mentioned the corset as a guess, but now he felt he had hit home.

"If you was my wife," he went on, "I'd certainly be real proud of your body. You're a damn fine good-lookin' woman. You'd make a preacher lay his Bible down. Why, ma'am, I'd want the whole town to know it. I'd even hire a brass band to parade in front of you on your way to church so's to git the whole town ready to know you're comin'. Look at that white lace dress you're wearin'! Look at those lips, all full an' red, without any paint! A woman like you needs a better settin'. Why, if I had my way, I'd take you to San Francisco an' put you in a barouche with a pair of matched bays, with two footmen in the back! I'd take you to Paris an' make them Frenchwomen sit up an' take notice. They'd jus' sit an' bite off their fingernails, they'd be so jealous! Yes, ma'am, I purely would like that."

All the time he was speaking he stared frankly at her breasts. She folded her arms in an instinctive gesture of rebuff, but this made him grin. She flushed and brought her arms down.

He swung his horse out of the way. She drove away. He watched her. Her back was rigid.

Two days later Cameron told him that she had left for a two-week visit back east with her family, and also to buy some furniture and a wardrobe. None of this surprised Slocum. He knew that moody, unhappy women were given to submerging their sorrow and bitterness in buying splurges. He was all for it. With Mrs. Hamilton out of town it would go all the better for him; he could concentrate on his bullion robbery. And she could spend the time on the slow railroad trip to the east and back to Socorro thinking about him.

16

A week later he casually mentioned to Morgan and the desk clerk at the hotel that he had to go to Chicago to straighten out his recently widowed sister's tangled legal business.

By then he had arranged to meet Cameron ten days later near the proposed ambush site.

He left on the morning train and arrived several hours later at Albuquerque. He bought a ticket for Chicago. He was pleased to see that the waiting room was full of people waiting for the eastbound train. A little conversation with the ticket agent had placed his presence firmly in that gentleman's memory. He quietly drifted out just before the train arrived, and once out of sight, tore up his ticket into small bits and threw them away in a small trash fire some shopkeeper had going in a vacant lot.

He had not been in Albuquerque for years. No one recognized him. The town was packed with people: cattlemen, cowboys and prospectors coming and going from the recent gold strikes up along the San Juan.

Heavy wagons creaked and swayed along the streets, sending up clouds of choking white dust. Dogs barked frantically at the huge dray horses. Indians in blankets moved impassively along the sidewalks, their glittering black eyes taking in everything above their impassive brown faces. Mexican-Americans in ponchos and the conical-topped sombreros typical of Chihuahua drifted indolently, smoking small brown cigars. Pueblo Indians sat immobile on the railroad station platform, waiting to sell hand-carved Kachinas to whatever tourists might happen along.

He bought two shotguns, ammunition, secondhand clothes which would fit both him and Cameron; boots for them both. He bought two horses, not much good, seeing he would shortly be killing them, but good enough. He bought ten burros. He bought two old saddles and saddle blankets, and all the necessary horse gear. He bought everything secondhand. This was no problem, since hundreds of disgusted prospectors were continually selling their equipment. He bought enough oats to keep the burros in good condition. He intended to push them fast across the desert and didn't want to waste time while they sought out their usual isolated patches to graze in. He bought some canned goods, a frying pan and a big slab of bacon. He carefully packed his good clothes in the valise he had brought up from Socorro. Late that afternoon he struck out to the southwest.

There was one man in the town who knew him. This was Henry Barrett, the assayer. He was a gray-bearded, small man, with a silvery voice and a personality tough as a pine knot. Slocum knew him well. Barrett could be counted upon to keep a secret. Slocum did not intend to give him any, but Barrett was no fool. He had the admirable habit of keeping his mouth shut whenever he discovered anything interesting by the use of inductive logic. He was very good at this; one of his habits was to play chess with anyone who happened to enter his office. He always won.

Barrett had enlisted in the war as a volunteer from his native Pennsylvania. He was a sergeant when he was badly wounded outside of Staunton in the Valley of Virginia. He had crawled to a farmhouse and was begging for water when a guerilla detachment trotted up. They sat Barrett against the barn and were about to bayonet him when Slocum rode up, knocked the bayonets up and curtly ordered them off the premises. Slocum could not spare any men to guard prisoners so he put Barrett in the farmer's wagon and left him on the outskirts of town, where he knew the man would shortly be found by a Northern cavalry patrol.

Years later, when Slocum was passing through Albuquerque, Barrett hailed him with delight.

Yes, Slocum thought, if things went well, he would be doing business soon with the admirably close-mouthed Mr. Barrett.

The rendezvous with Cameron was a well-watered-and-grassed box canyon five miles north of the Socorro-Black Mountain road. Slocum reached it six days later. All the stock was in good condition. He had let them move slowly, grazing as they went. They arrived rested and well fed. He hobbled them and turned them all loose to graze. He had seen no one during the six days. He hoped he hadn't been seen, although in Indian country one never knew.

Cameron was waiting. He had hobbled his horse, and he had dumped his saddle on the ground, spread the blanket and was leaning back against the saddle, smoking. He was in a bad mood. He had forgotten that at high altitudes it was much colder at night than in Socorro, and his thin coat had not been of much help during the previous night. He had not dared to light a fire—this act Slocum considered unusually intelligent for Cameron—and he had been unable to sleep. He kept yawning and nodding impatiently as Slocum greeted him.

Slocum decided to be quiet. He handed over the secondhand clothes he had bought for Cameron back in Albuquerque, and watched the man change. Cameron wore an old undershirt gray with dirt. He never wore underpants. Slocum hoped the man would fall into some creek somewhere; the accident might improve his aroma.

Cameron had ridden out from Socorro the night before. He was ravenous. Slocum knew how to make a small fire that would produce hardly any smoke. He collected some pieces of hardwood by grubbing up some mesquite roots with his pick. The smoke rose only a few feet before it was dissipated by the wind coming off the mountain slopes. He fried bacon and heated up a can of beans. Cameron ate in huge gulps. Between bites he mentioned that the burros looked like they had wintered on pine cones.

"I thought you'd feel better after you et," Slocum said genially, "an' not be so cantankerous. Nothin' wrong with the burros."

Cameron grunted.

"How they gonna look when we're haulin' ass acrost the desert?" he demanded.

"Got oats," Slocum said.

Cameron was silent. Slocum looked at him calmly. The damn fool, he thought—here we are about to rob us a stagecoach with armed guards on it and maybe make ourselves enough to retire on the rest of our lives—and here he is picking and nagging like a sour old woman.

They passed the night comfortably enough, with the extra blankets Slocum had brought along. At sunrise they ate three-day-old biscuits and two apples apiece. Slocum considered it too risky to light a fire on the same day of the robbery.

They took the burros and the horses over to the little clearing in which they had sat in the buggy almost a month before. They spoke very little. Cameron was nervous and irritable. Slocum, as he usually was before action, was calm and smiling. A little before the sun reached its zenith, Cameron scrambled down from the top of the ridge behind the clearing.

"There she is!" he yelled. "She jus' come over the ridge acrost the valley! Let's go!"

"Take it easy," Slocum said. "We got plenty of time."

He lit a cigar and puffed calmly. They were standing behind a screen of low-growing pines. They could see the coach bouncing across the flat valley land. Then it disappeared as it swung in a big curve to make an approach up the mountain by an easy grade. Slocum mounted and took several drags from the cigar. When it was almost all burned, he pinched it out and carefully dropped it onto level rock. He pushed his bandanna up till his face was covered, and sat easily, balancing his shotgun across his saddle horn.

Cameron began biting his lips. He turned to look at Slocum and stared in astonishment, for Slocum was occupied in seeing if he could find the center of balance of the shotgun atop the horn. Cameron's horse quickly sensed his rider's nervousness and promptly began exhibiting signs of it as well. In order to control the animal, Cameron doubled the reins in his left hand and slashed the horse across the face. Slocum cursed under his breath and hoped that Cameron wouldn't do anything foolish before the stagecoach would arrive.

With a sigh of relief Slocum heard the rumble of wheels and the creaking of the springs. Then it appeared through the branches, moving at a walking pace. There were no passengers. The two guards were walking beside it, cradling their Winchesters in their elbows. They were sweating. One man was fanning himself with his hat.

"Look at them springs!" Cameron hissed in Slocum's ear. "All flattened out."

"Yeah. Very nice."

"I certainly pick 'em!"

When the coach was 15 feet away Slocum said, "Now."

Their horses slid down the slight slope and into the road. Cameron covered the driver; Slocum's shotgun muzzle described small circles around the two guards. They started to pull their Winchesters into firing position.

"Don't!" Slocum barked, in a flat, nasal tone unlike his usual soft speech. "You'll come apart, fellers." He cocked both barrels. At the sound of the dry clicks both men froze.

"Wrap the lines around the brake an' get down, driver!"

The driver hesitated. One hand strayed near the carbine on the seat beside him. From the corner of one eye, Slocum saw Cameron swinging his shotgun up at the driver's face. With his left hand Slocum struck the barrel upward just in time. The tremendous blast of both barrels set the horses to plunging. In that narrow place the crash was ear-splitting, literally; Slocum winced with the pain. The guards automatically grabbed for the horses' bridles. A rain of pine needles and shreds of bark fell upon the driver and his horses. The smell of gunpowder mingled with that of the pine needles. The driver got down, shaking.

"Reload, you dumb sonofabitch!" Slocum muttered furiously.

Cameron ejected the shells and slid in new ones, glaring in hatred at Slocum. Slocum knew the driver could have been controlled without killing him. Still, the blast had frightened the three men into immediate compliance. They were not likely to cause any more trouble.

"Unbuckle your belts!"

The gun belts dropped.

"Take off your boots." The three men kicked them off.

"You ain't gonna get away with this," one of the guards said.

"Start walkin' back," Slocum ordered. "An' remember, we c'n see you a long, long ways. Start!"

The three men began to pick their way painfully over the ruts and pebbles.

Slocum waited till the men had descended around the first bend in the road. He mounted the stagecoach, unwrapped the lines and drove it off the road till it was hidden behind the screen of pines. In the boot under the driver's seat and inside the coach between the two seats were the gold bars. He had never before seen so much gold at one time. He enjoyed the sensation for a few seconds. Then he bent down to pick them up. Straightening up with one in his hands, he saw the naked lust blazing in Cameron's face.

Working quickly, they managed to lash them on the burros in 20 minutes.

Slocum jumped up on the seat, grabbed the guard's carbine and jumped down. He killed each horse with one bullet through the brain. He left all the carbines and the gun belts inside the coach. He didn't need them and he saw no reason why the three men couldn't get them back eventually, although the horses would be stinking up the air horribly if the buzzards didn't get to them first.

They started. First they edged out of the pine slopes. Far down in the valley they could just make out the three tiny figures trudging painfully back towards the Dirty Dog mine.

Lashed head to tail the ten burros followed the two men as they set out across the lava beds. Three hours later, pushing as hard as they could, they came out to the beginning of the desert. First, there was a wide, shallow river to wade across. They watered all the stock leisurely, filled their canvas water bags and then Slocum pitched the two shotguns into the middle of the river. The muddy brown current revealed nothing.

"Now we ride hard!" said Cameron.

"Right," said Slocum. "We push leather."

17

Two nights later they were 50 miles to the northwest, deep in a country of wide, flat mesas covered with scrub chapparal and little valleys filled with grotesque wind-carved red rock formations, rising each in isolation from the plain, like chess pieces on a board. Long slopes pitched gently upwards to the foot of the mesas. The soil was too dry for grass, except for isolated patches near subterranean springs or wherever a trickle of water seeped down from a mesa.

The country could not even support small flocks of sheep. The result—good for Slocum and Cameron—was that even sheepmen would have nothing to do with it; even the Navajos preferred the higher country to the west, where the altitude caught the moisture-filled winds and forced them to drop their rain.

Here it was barren. And this was precisely why Slocum had chosen it for an escape route.

He knew where he could find water each night. He pushed hard for another day, late into the afternoon. By then they were 80 miles away. Slocum was now sure that they had shaken off all pursuit. It was about time, he thought. Neither he nor Cameron trusted the other, and they had had very little sleep.

Early in the morning they had come across a maverick calf, far from its range and without its mother. They butchered it and took some ribs along. That night it would be safe to make a fire.

"What say we divvy up an' then eat a good supper outta them ribs?" asked Cameron during the noon halt.

"Good idea."

So they stopped late that afternoon. They took off the packs. The concentrated weight of the gold had rubbed the burros' backs raw, but Slocum had foreseen this and had brought along some ointment he had picked up at a veterinary's. He stood and rubbed the ointment into the burros while he watched Cameron spread two blankets and divide up the bullion, 70-30.

Cameron's head oscillated slowly as he looked at each pile in turn. From time to time his heavy head swung around and looked at Slocum. He was sitting cross-legged, his shoulders slumped with exhaustion. He was trying to conceal his disgust with the percentage agreement but he was not a good actor. Slocum did not like to turn his back and tried to arrange his cooking so that he would not have to.

"Look at that pile," Cameron said suddenly. "It's so big it would sweat a danged rat to run around it."

He took a branch, peeled it, sharpened it and ran it through some ribs. He propped it up near the fire and salted it. He opened a can of beans and set it in the coals and then boiled coffee.

"A man eats pretty good travelin' with you, Sheridan," Cameron growled. Slocum shrugged. Cameron rolled a cigarette. "We pulled that off pretty nice," he went on. "Went like clockwork. Nothin' went wrong. What say you an' me, we throw in together, permanentlike? I know where there's four bushels of gold buried in the Nations. 'Course, they're buried in someone's house." He grinned, sniffing the ribs hungrily. "We might have to use a shotgun or two to take 'em out. Shame you threw 'em away." His face clouded.

Slocum said nothing. This was the kind of pointless and stupid nagging he could not abide.

The idea of throwing in with Cameron filled Slocum with loathing.

"Mebbe," he said judiciously, as if he were seriously considering the suggestion. He turned the ribs.

"Them calf ribs shore smell nice," Cameron said, hitching closer to the fire.

Slocum turned some more ribs to broil the other

side. This movement gave him an opportunity to turn his face away from Cameron, who was grinning. Now that he was rich he was beginning to reminisce about Indian women.

"Hell, they'd toss their shoes under your bed for an ole pair of socks," he said. "Or for a bag o' Bull Durham.

"Hell, when you was gone to Albuquerque some miners come in an' said when they was ridin' in from the Dirty Dog, they smelt mescal roots them 'paches was cookin' an' storin' up. The smell came right down a canyon. Guess them 'paches forgot that smell could carry so far. Got careless. So they hightailed it to Socorro an' told me. One of them miners climbed a hill an' said it was a band of mebbe six or seven. So I got together 'bout fifteen guys an' we rode all day an' crawled up on 'em after dark. They was still roastin' mescal an' we jumped 'em at sunrise.

"They was an ole man an' two ole women an' one gall half-bellied out. She'd pop in a couple months. There was two kids. We kilt 'em all."

"The kids, too?"

"Yeah."

"And the pregnant girl?"

"Nits become lice," Cameron said indifferently. "The gal ran up the hill, but I got my hoss an' cut 'er off. That made 'er mine, y'see. The others didn't think of headin' 'er off with a hoss. She backed off 'gainst a tree. I reached down to grab 'er but the brown bitch went at me with a knife. So I shot 'er in the belly."

"Then?"

"She sat down an' began howlin' somethin'."

It would be her death song, Slocum knew. "An' then what happened?" He pretended great interest. His face was convulsed with loathing, but his back was to Cameron.

"Them ribs sure is great," Cameron said. "You c'n

cook for me anytime." He reached across and hacked off several more.

"Yeah, what happened next. Yeah, I shot 'er again. This time she fell over on 'er side, kerplunk! I pulled 'er dress off. I woulda screwed 'er, she had good tits, but she was too bloody."

"Then?"

"I jus' let 'er lay, but I wanted a souvenir. So I got this. It was hangin' to her belt." Cameron got up, smearing his hands across his pants. He pulled something from his saddlebag and tossed it over the fire to Slocum.

When Slocum looked at it he knew Cameron had to die.

It was a buckskin pouch with the letter *S* worked on it in tiny blue beads.

18

Cameron sat cross-legged, gnawing at the ribs. From time to time he lifted his shaggy head from the food and stared at the neatly stacked ingots glowing in the firelight. Then he swung his head around and grinned at Slocum, who was sitting silently across from him, staring down at the beaded buckskin pouch in his hands.

" 'At's only the beginnin'," he boasted. "You an' me, Sheridan, we're gonna run the whole country. Yessir, from the Missouri to the Rockies. The two of us!"

Slocum slowly realized the man had been drinking. It was typical of Cameron that he had been secretly taking nips from his saddlebag and didn't offer any to Slocum. It was also typical of his inconsistency that he was boasting of their future partnership while he was keeping the whiskey to himself. Now that Cameron was rich all his thoughts were on whiskey, women and ribs. Cameron took another bite and wiped his greasy palms across his facial stubble. This filthy habit made his face glisten in the firelight.

"I bet if I showed that Hamilton bitch some of this here gold she'd be fast enough shuckin' off her purty white lace dress," he mumbled. "I bet she married 'im 'cause he musta told 'er he was a big rancher or somethin' like that. No ways else for 'er to stick 'erself in a town like Socorro. Jus' let 'er get a peep at some o' that gold an' she'd shuck off 'er dress lickety-split. Wanna bet?"

It was time to kill Cameron.

Slocum carefully put down his coffee cup. He leaned forward and rubbed his palms back and forth on the dirt to get the grease off. He didn't want his right hand to slip on the silver inlays which were shining now like little patches of the moon. Cameron looked at him, puzzled at Slocum's impassive face and the rubbing of his hands in the dirt.

Slocum leaned forward and put a palm on each of his knees.

"I don't think I'm the right man for all that," he said slowly.

"Yeah? Why not?" Cameron demanded, tearing away the meat from the bones.

"Because my name is John Slocum."

For about three seconds there was no response. It took that long for the sentence to sink into Cameron's alcohol-blurred mind.

When it finally reached home, Cameron's response was better than Slocum would have guessed. Cameron kept on chewing and swallowing.

"Aw, quit it. You don't look nothin' like John." He laughed.

"That's 'cause I'm clean-shaved, Cameron. You jus'

lean back an' imagine me with stubble and a heavy mustache. Imagine me with my red sash. An' with a heavy sunburn. Keep imaginin', you sonofabitch!"

Slocum felt his patience running away from him. He was afraid that his aim would be spelled if he really let go with his pent-up hatred.

"Now look here, you ain't got no call——"

"Where's your red suspenders, Cameron? I know you, you cheap bastard. You're afraid to wear 'em, an' you're too cheap to throw 'em away."

That was two curses no Westerner would stand for. And now Cameron had to know for sure that it was really John Slocum who was sitting across the fire. But all Cameron did was toss his bones in the fire.

"If she looks good to you," Slocum said thickly, "I'll be glad to give it a whirl. What say?"

Cameron disappointed him. "We make a good team, Johnny," Cameron said. "Mebbe I did wrong. But we work real good together. What say we make the split eighty-twenty? Sort of lettin' me make up for it.

"An' when we git back to Socorro," Cameron went on, "I'll find out when the next shipment is comin' down from the Dirty Dog. An' you an' me, why, we'll take 'em again. To show you I really wanna show I'm sorry, we'll split that one eighty-twenty—in *your* favor. How you gonna beat *that?*"

Slocum said nothing. He was taking long deep breaths to control his rage before it would get out of control. And if he were to go out of control, the advantage would immediately pass to Cameron.

Cameron was emboldened by Slocum's silence, which he took to mean agreement. He pressed his argument more forcefully.

"An' after that, we'll share an' share alike. In a couple years, why, John, we'll git more famous than the James boys! Then we c'n take it easy the rest of our lives an' just lay back in the shade an' smoke seegars. What say, John?"

He leaned forward eagerly, balancing himself with his fingertips spread apart on the ground, near the fire.

Slocum didn't like it at all, but Cameron's strategy had paid off. Slocum was so sure that Cameron was sincere in his proposal that he had relaxed a little.

Cameron suddenly grabbed two burning embers and flung them directly at Slocum's face. At the same time he rolled sidewards. Slocum jerked his Colt and fired, but since he had flung up his left hand to protect his eyes he missed the shot.

Cameron was now somewhere in the dark. Slocum knew he was aiming at him. He knew he had to move fast. Just as he got to his knees Cameron fired. The bullet passed under his arm, slicing open his shirt and searing the skin. Slocum fired at the flash, but Cameron kept moving. He was invisible, completely out of the range of the firelight. Slocum rolled over and ran at a crouch until he, too, was in the blackness. He sat down and pulled off his boots. He remembered the lesson Nachodise had given him. He was going to stalk Cameron like an Indian. He crouched low, so that his body wouldn't blot out any stars and so provide a target for Cameron, who, if he had any sense, was at that very second lying flat and waiting for some such move.

He began moving very slowly towards where he had last seen the flash of Cameron's Colt. He felt with his toes for a flat surface without any pebbles. When he found it he put his foot down very slowly. He repeated the process several times, listening with all his might for the slightest sound in Cameron's direction. He knew the man could move quickly and quietly when he wished.

Slocum had only gone four feet when he heard a

gasp and a terrified moan wrenched out of Cameron's mouth. The sound came from 30 feet away. Slocum held his fire.

"John, John!" the man called in terror.

Cameron liked to play games. Slocum was wary. He made no move or sound. He very quietly stretched flat on the ground to make even less of a target against the star-filled sky.

A massive brown rope flowed by him. By now Slocum's sight had adjusted to the starlight. The spade-shaped head was as big as his hand. He recognized the typical markings of a diamondback rattlesnake. It was one of the biggest Slocum had ever seen. With that enormous head it would generate an enormous amount of venom. He didn't move. In a few seconds the big snake had vanished into a clump of cholla, leaving behind its peculiar musty odor.

"John, I got bit!"

Slocum pressed flat to the ground. He formed a megaphone with his hands and spoke to one side in order to confuse Cameron as to direction if he would be up to any tricks.

"Throw your gun towards me," he said.

The Colt thudded near him.

"Stand up with your hands in the air."

"Sure, John, sure!"

A tall figure loomed up suddenly, 15 feet away.

"Move to the fire and strip."

"But——"

"Strip!"

Slocum wasn't taking any chances that all this might be a clever act, and that the man would intend to knife him when he got close.

Cameron moved to the fire and began to frantically pull off his clothes. Then he stood naked.

Slocum didn't move.

"John, do somethin'!"

Now Slocum was sure that Cameron had been bitten. He recognized the symptoms of shock. But he decided to be wary nevertheless. Cameron had shown himself to be much smarter than Slocum had ever known him to be and always capable of surprising him. But this was natural, Slocum thought: He had had Cameron recommended to him, and the train robbery was the first job they had ever been on together.

He was never to be trusted again. Even if he had been bitten, it might be on a calf or ankle. A few swift slashes with his knife and Cameron would be all right.

Slocum moved closer, keeping the muzzle of his Colt pointed at Cameron's stomach.

He stopped four feet away. Cameron was facing the fire directly.

"Where?" Slocum asked.

Cameron placed a dirty forefinger on his neck. Slocum saw the jugular vein, and right in the middle of it were two tiny punctures, each with a drop of blood oozing from it.

This was no trick. Slocum holstered his gun and sat down across the fire.

"John, do somethin' fast!"

"All I'm gonna do is look at you," Slocum said. He felt embittered. The man was going to die and Slocum would not be responsible. He could not even take vengeance for Idagalele and her unborn child.

"John, please, *please!*"

"You want me to put a tourniquet on your throat, for crissake? If the rattler used up his poison on a rabbit or somethin' before he got to you, you'll live. If he didn't, why, you bastard, you're dead. Sit down an' wait."

Cameron slid to his knees. A sweat had covered him completely, in spite of the chill night air. He opened his mouth and leaned forward. Long bloody ropes of saliva dangled from his mouth. So the diamondback had delivered a full load. His heart was pumping furiously in his terror, spreading the poison quickly. His chest heaved like a bellows gone mad. Slocum stared at him. He felt no pity. He hoped that Idagalele was enjoying the spectacle in whatever heaven was hers.

"Gimme yore knife, John!" Cameron wanted to cut open the punctures.

Slocum shook his head.

"Please, *please!* You c'n take my share. All of it, John!"

Slocum said nothing.

By a superhuman effort Cameron heaved his naked body to his feet. He took an unsteady step towards Slocum. He tripped on a stone and fell headlong. He struggled to his knees and sobbing, began to crawl once more towards Slocum.

The bullet from Cameron's own Colt exploded in the hard-packed desert soil a foot from Cameron's face. Gravel sprayed upward and blood began to flow from myriad tiny cuts. Dust was embedded in his eyes, and he paused to rub them with his filthy hands.

Years ago, in the Sonoran desert, Slocum had been bitten by a sidewinder. It had been in the forearm. Luckily, it was a small snake but nevertheless, the pain had been excruciating, as if someone were twisting white-hot pokers in and out of his arm. The poison had spread quickly, even though Slocum had gashed open the puncture marks and had sucked out most of the poison within 30 seconds. The pain had moved up his arm, across both shoulders and then seemed to cascade down his entire torso. The agony had increased as the poison moved along its foreordained path.

Cameron was going through it now, but in far more

intense fashion. He clasped himself with both arms and then bent over groaning, bending his body till his forehead touched the ground. When he paused for breath, Slocum could hear his blood dripping onto the dry ground, which seemed to Slocum to suck it up greedily, as if it wanted more.

"You're dyin', Cameron," Slocum said.

"John, shoot me!"

"No. I want to watch this all the way, you rotten bastard!"

Blood had begun to ooze from his mouth and nostrils. He put his hands to his throat and pressed in. The pain was beginning to be unbearable. Blood began to leak from his rectum. Suddenly he became unconscious.

Slocum stood up, wary lest this might be a trick. He stood back of Cameron, pointed the Colt at his head and pulled open an eyelid. The eye stared up at him, unseeing. He let the eyelid fall. Bloody saliva oozed from the mouth and nose.

Slocum suddenly slapped Cameron's face as hard as he could.

"Wake up, you bastard, oh you bastard," he muttered. "Wake up. Wake up, you dirty bastard!" He punched him in the mouth as hard as he could. He broke several teeth and cut his knuckles, but Cameron was in a coma and dying. In three minutes his breathing became erratic, raced and suddenly stopped.

Well, Slocum thought, that's the end of number one.

19

Slocum couldn't sleep. He sat up all night, feeding the fire and drinking Cameron's whiskey. Occasionally he lifted his head and stared at Cameron's body. The neck had swollen to twice its normal size and had turned black. The tongue, too, had turned black, twice its normal size. It was too big for the mouth to hold it, and it protruded through the broken teeth. From time to time Slocum splashed a little whiskey on his bloody knuckles.

When there was enough light he stood up and looked at the ingots. Cameron's one wild shot had gone on to gouge out a groove the length of the topmost ingot, as if this last violent gesture of his life was designed by him to leave his mark on both his enemy and the treasure whose theft he had engineered.

He took a pick and shovel and buried the gold midway between the two oldest cottonwoods, far enough back from the creek so that the hole would be far above the spring flood line. He spread the excavated dirt on a saddle blanket and threw it into the river, following it with Cameron's Colt and carbine. Afterwards he dragged a branch back and forth over the hole and littered the area with fallen leaves. There would be no way of knowing that the area had ever been disturbed.

He kept out four ingots.

He left the body where it lay. With the first light he had noticed several tiny black objects circling lazily high overhead. By the time Slocum would make his noon halt, all that would be left of Cameron would be a skeleton.

At the noon halt he burned Cameron's clothes and his saddle and boots. In the saddlebag he found a full bottle of bourbon. At the edge of the first barranca he killed Cameron's horse with one shot and pushed it over. Within minutes buzzards had settled on it.

He could have gotten $50 for it in Fort Wingate, but questions might come up how come he had an extra horse. And a man with $2 million could afford to be generous with death.

When night came he halted. He wasn't hungry but

he forced himself to fry bacon and drink coffee. During the night he wasn't able to sleep. He sat up and drank Cameron's last bottle. Then he stretched out on his bedroll with his hands clasped behind his head. His Colt was shoved, as always, under the saddle he used for a pillow.

He was drunk and he knew it. He had $2 million. The man who had betrayed him was dead. Yet he took no satisfaction from the fact, since he knew that he was not directly responsible for it. He would have to work things out better with number two.

The night sky began to pale. Then the sun soared over the eastern horizon and up through the tangled ocotillo. Its color changed from orange to the hot glowing white it would be till sunset. It was going to be another hot day.

It was time to get moving. He fed the burros and his horse, watered them, saddled up and led out the string of burros. A sudden thought came to him.

Some day someone would find Cameron's bullet. It would have its nose coated with gold. And the finder would never be able to guess why.

Slocum smiled for the first time in days.

20

In six days he was back in Albuquerque, wearing the clothes he had started out in from Socorro three weeks ago. He had disposed of his stock in Fort Wingate with a good profit, since the resent gold strike on the San Juan had created a big demand for good burros—and his were in top condition. No one noticed him in Fort Wingate, since the little town was full of miners coming in from the Nevada and Montana diggings.

All the way back to Albuquerque he sat, figuring out how to handle the sale of the bullion. Any such large amount dumped on the market at once would attract a lot of attention, most of it bound to be unpleasant. It had to be fed into it in dribbles. When he swung off the train he had made his plans.

He walked into Henry Barrett's office. The assayer had come west in his early 20s, bitten by gold fever. He had never struck it rich. He went back east, studied chemistry at Columbia, and this time went out west knowing he could always make a decent living around his favorite metal and would never have to live again on cold flapjacks and soggy bacon. Since his interests in every other field never coincided with anyone else's in the usual frontier towns where he set up his office, with its retorts and glass flasks and demijohns filled with acids, he had learned how to play chess. He was always looking for a good player. Failing that, he always played the great games of chess history, walking from one side of the board to the other. Some people thought he was slightly mad, but Slocum had never made that mistake.

Besides chess, he only cared about the quality of the gold offered him. Nothing else. When Slocum placed the three ingots in front of him on the counter his eyes opened wide. He took a small flat black stone and rubbed it on one corner of the ingot. A thin hairline of gold transferred itself to the stone. Barrett set the stone down and carefully opening a vial of nitric acid, poured a drop on the gold scratch.

It remained unchanged. Satisfied, Barrett tested the other two ingots. They tested out gold. Then he weighed them. Slocum watched Barrett smiling as he worked.

"Like assaying?"

"No," Barrett said. "What I *like* is gold. I mean, I *love* gold. And don't misunderstand me. I don't love it because it's valuable. It's a noble metal. It's more malleable than any other metal; I can beat it into leaves one two-hundred-and-fifty-thousandths of an inch thick. That means, in case you're not too sure what I mean, I can put a quarter of a million of those leaves one on top of the other and when I get them all together, why, it'll only make a pile one inch thick. And it's the most ductile of metals; *that* means I can take one grain of it and draw it out into a wire five hundred and one feet long. Not to mention it never rusts. I can bury one of those ingots and come back five, fifty, one hundred, two thousand, five thousand years later and dig it up—and it'll be as bright as the day I buried it. Yes. I love it."

Slocum had felt his heart jump when Barrett had mentioned burying the ingots, but he decided that it was simply a coincidence.

"What do you offer?"

"Market price," Barrett said.

"Done."

He watched as Barrett immediately set the ingots in the furnace. He knew that Barrett suspected the source and wanted to destroy their distinctive shapes as soon as possible.

"Got any more?"

"Maybe. How much can you use?"

"As much as you give me."

"A lot more?"

Barrett looked up. The man had a brow ridge which extended far out above his eyes. It gave his face a hooded effect, as if he were a hawk that had suddenly become man-sized.

Slocum had noticed a poster in the post office offering a $5000 reward for information leading to the capture of the two stagecoach robbers who had seized the Dirty Dog mine shipment. Sheriff Andy Hamilton, Socorro, Territory of New Mexico, was to be notified. The reward was being offered by the mine operators. Cheap bastards, Slocum thought. The men wore old red bandannas, brown boots run down at the heels, one of them wore cheap Mexican spurs and both were carrying shotguns. One of them spoke in a gruff voice and had green eyes.

All of that material had been burned or thrown into the river, Slocum thought, with a pleased sensation. The cheap Mexican spurs belonged to Cameron, who liked to mercilessly rowel his horses with them. Slocum had tossed them into the river. He had assumed the gruff voice when he was doing the talking. The only thing he could not have concealed was the color of his eyes. But there were plenty of green-eyed men floating around New Mexico. As a matter of fact, many purebred Mexicans, of Spanish lineage, had green eyes, and they did not take kindly to American exploitation of the mineral rights which had been Mexican for over 300 years. So the search would not be limited to Anglos. Good.

Barrett was talking.

"Beg your pardon?"

"I said I can use a lot more."

Slocum did some fast mental arithmetic. Five thousand dollars was very good pay for just dropping in across the street and quietly sending a telegram down to Socorro. But if Barrett could get the idea he could make a lot more by handling all the gold Slocum would bring him, he'd keep his mouth shut. And Slocum believed in persuading people they would make good money and live longer as well, if they'd see eye to eye with him.

"I could bring some in from time to time," Slocum said easily. "I'm workin' on the richest damn bonanza you ever saw. Just pick up the quartz and it crumbles in your hand like a butter cookie. Just pick out them little nuggets, size of grains of rice, sometimes bigger. Never saw anythin' like it in my life."

Slocum could see the curiosity developing in the

hooded face. Barrett, it was clear to Slocum, had been skeptical about the source of the ingots; that explained his haste to melt it down. But now, Slocum felt, the man was not so sure. The old gold lust had worked its magic: Barrett *wanted* to believe any romantic story about his favorite object. Slocum, watching Barrett's face narrowly, decided to feed his curiosity. He knew it would not go further; the man was well known for keeping his mouth as grimly clamped down as a snapping turtle.

Besides, there was Barrett's gratitude to play upon. He had never forgotten that Slocum had saved his life from the guerrillas that day outside Staunton. Yes, there was a good chance that Barrett would keep his mouth shut.

"I didn't stumble across an outcrop," Slocum said. "Wasn't like Comstock out there near Virginia City. Helped out an old Indian who was starvin', helped out his squaw. So he just took me to show me one of them old Spanish mines they covered up when the Apaches got rough 'bout a hundred years ago. I just grubbed out the trees an' brush an' there she was. Suppose every month or so I come in with, say, twenty, thirty ingots."

Barrett let out a long amazed whistle. "That's a *lot* of money for me to get up."

"You bet. So let's say you just pay me three dollars an ounce less than the market. Sort of an inducement for you."

Barrett stared at him. He would make his regular profit as usual, by paying the market price—but Slocum's offer meant he would make almost $50 extra for every pound that Slocum would deliver.

"How many pounds you figure you'll bring in?"

"Couldn't tell just right now. She's runnin' very rich. Did some sample drillin'. Ever' goddamn vein is six–seven feet thick. Ore's so rich you c'n pick out little nuggets with your fingernail. An' a couple little cricks been runnin' down the mountain, why, they been carryin' this stuff a couple thousand, million years, an' them cricks got them cracks down in bedrock, an' the cracks is jus' jam full of gold. *Solid.* We don' have to pan the stuff out. You c'n jus' pull off your boots an' pants, sit on the bottom, an' jus' keep chunkin' nuggets into the pan like you was pickin' strawberries."

Barrett stared at him enviously. Slocum was a good liar, and he had worked himself so deeply into his story that he temporarily believed it while he was telling it. His face was flushed with excitement and sincerity.

"The Lord giveth and the Lord taketh away," Barrett said, shrugging. "And in none of it is there rhyme or reason." He was content. He could see no traps being baited for him.

"So," Slocum went on, "next trip, I'll be bringin' in, oh, say six hundred pounds."

Six hundred pounds. Besides his ordinary profit, that meant $3000 extra to Barrett. The next trip after that—if the weight would be the same—would bring him another extra $3000.

That was a big inducement, Slocum knew, to play along with him. That made, already, a total of one thousand dollars more than the reward. All he had to do was promise several more shipments. He would have a very closemouthed assayer in Albuquerque bound to him by that very strong link: financial profit.

He deposited $48,000 in the Merchants and Cattlemen's Bank under the name of Cameron Hendricks. It was the least he could do.

21

Late that afternoon Slocum dropped off the train at Socorro. He walked away from the depot and up the two dusty blocks to his hotel. Tompkins was sitting at the desk playing solitaire with a filthy old deck.

"Afternoon," he said. "Kept your room f'r ye. How's the trip?"

"Hot, dirty, I got covered with ashes an' soot. Glad to be back here."

"Took a train ride oncet in August. Only a thin sheet of sandpaper between that day coach an' hell. Things goin' all right back in Chicago?"

Slocum shrugged. "Settlin' an estate, movin' my sister and her kids to a new house—not somethin' a man likes to think back on."

"Reckon so. Think she'll be all right?"

"Her no-good husband died just about broke. I'll have to help out till the kids get older. Let me have my key, Mr. Tompkins."

"Sure." Tompkins made no move for the key. He shuffled the cards together, placed the deck to one side and leaned forward on his elbows. Slocum sighed inwardly. The old man wanted to gossip. He resigned himself to it with a good grace; Tompkins was a reliable gossip columnist.

"Lots of excitement while you was gone. Two men robbed the bullion stage comin' down from the Dirty Dog. Got clean away with two hunnerd thousand dollars' worth."

"They get 'em?"

"Nope."

"Anyone losin' sleep here?"

Tompkins grinned. "Can't say that fer a fact. No widder woman's gonna starve. Lots more gold where that come from. Sheriff's all het up 'cause the mine people say he lost the trail out on the lava beds. They tole 'im he couldn't find his nose on a dark night usin' both hands. He sounds like he got a contract to do all the swearin' in the Territory. Two o' his deppities quit. He's like a dog run over by a wagon—keeps bitin' hisself an' anyone in reach. No call to talk like that to anyone."

It gave Slocum a small pleasant feeling to realize that Hamilton's death would probably bring him a vote of thanks from the entire county. But he must not seem too interested in the robbery. But Tompkins went back to it.

"Two hunnerd thousand," he mused. "My. That could buy a man a powerful amount of whiskey."

Dirty lying bastards, Slocum thought. He was half-amused, half-irritated at the mine owners. He didn't understand how their minds worked. By playing down the amount stolen, did they hope to make other possible robbers think that they wouldn't stand to gain a lot if they took a crack at the next shipment? Was the lie to make the eastern stockholders feel better? The mine owners could always doctor the books and make up for the loss on subsequent shipments.

Slocum despised the conniving minds of men in finance. They could always recoup their losses and survive easily when Slocum would relieve them of their property, whether it be gold or cattle. And Slocum prided himself on the fact that he took terrible risks each time he sought to separate some gold or some white-faced Herefords from their rightful owners. He had, as it were, paid his dues. Always. And he had never driven a poor, hardworking squatter off his pitiful tiny ranch, nor had he hired professional gunmen to kill sheepmen in order to clear a range for cattle. Nor had he faked documents in order to supersede the original Spanish land grants, many of them 300 years old. Slocum knew that Morgan, whom he liked, had done such things. He despised such acts and held such people in contempt. Life became somewhat difficult when he found himself liking them if they were like Morgan.

He sighed. Tompkins was talking about Chicago. He told the old man about his imaginary dead sister's imaginary alcoholic husband. He hoped the story of his visit to Chicago would be spread all over Socorro by the Tompkins Daily Clarion-Bugle. Fine. He wanted people to believe he would need extra money to send back east to his sister. People would unconsciously refuse to entertain the thought that a man with $200,000 would come back to the scene of the robbery—not only that, they simply wouldn't buy the thought that he would then go to work every night gambling.

Now the old man had slipped the deck of cards into the desk drawer. He looked as if he intended to settle down into a long, comfortable chat, like an old lonely spinster. Slocum didn't like to hurt anyone's feelings needlessly. He stayed. Tompkins was rambling on again about the robbery.

Slocum asked, "Anybody get hurt?"

"Naw!"

"Well, then, God bless the robbers."

"Reckon you're right, Mr. Sheridan. Nobody got hurt 'cept the Dirty Dog an' they'll recover right quick. They pulled it right smart, them two fellers. Far better than the last time."

It would not do to show boredom at this point. Tompkins might gossip like a sex-starved schoolteacher in a one-room prairie schoolhouse, but he was no fool.

"Last time?"

"Yep. Mebbe four months ago. Three, four men tried to stick up the train goin' down to Las Cruces with a lot o' bullion in the express car. Somethin' went wrong. Mebbe their bowstrings was wet. They kilt one of the deppities."

"Damn shame," Slocum said sincerely.

"Mebbe the damn feller needed killin'," Tompkins said. "Some of them fellers hangin' out 'round the sheriff's office I wouldn't turn my back on nohow iffen I had two silver dollars rubbin' each other in my pocket."

Somehow those last sentences made Slocum feel somewhat better.

"But that five-thousand-dollar reward, now that's a right smart piece of change, son. Iffen I had it, I'd just hole up somewheres where it's warm all the year 'round, with a cellar full o' gallons of whiskey, and do a lot of readin'. No pints. No quarts. Just keep tippin' 'at ole gallon jug up like it was cider. Get an apple-country shoulder."

"I could use that reward myself," Slocum said, slowly shaking his head.

"Sure reckon you could, with your sister an' her kids an' all. But I tell you, mister, one o' them robbers is gonna get drunk in some saloon somewheres. He's gonna start braggin' how bad an' smart he is. An' whoever's lucky enough to be there with his ears wide open, why, that feller's gonna make hisself some easy money. Mark my words."

"Damn right." Slocum bent down to pick up his valise.

"An' it might be you."

Luckily, Slocum's head was averted. The sudden shock contorted his face and then left it as suddenly as a lightning flash. When he straightened up and faced Tompkins his face was in complete control. He looked puzzled.

"What?" he asked.

"Yep. You're in them saloons ev'ry night. You might hear this feller bullshittin' away. An' there's five thousand bucks in yore pocket, just as easy!"

"You're right. Never thought of that. I sure could *use* it."

"You bet, with your sister an' all," Tompkins said, with sympathy.

"Thank you, Mr. Tompkins. I'm mighty tired. Think I'll grab a little shut-eye."

He took the key and went to his room upstairs. It had not been swept and the window was closed. The room smelled stale. The windowsill was littered with dead flies. He opened the window, brushed the flies out into the street and saw Mrs. Hamilton going by in her sulky. The sound of the window opening had attracted her attention, and she looked up idly. Slocum leaned out, successfully drawing several glances of the passersby, and smiled. She whipped her head around, but Slocum was satisfied that the little byplay had been noticed.

Whistling now, he unbuckled his gun belt, slid out the Colt onto the bed and began to oil and clean it carefully. He took an old linen shirt from the bureau drawer and used it to wipe off the excess oil. He had cleaned it the morning after he had fired that one shot at Cameron in the dark, but he had been so angry at missing that he had rammed the patch through carelessly. This time he took his time in cleaning it. He knew that his life depended upon its functioning well. He might never need it for months, but when he would need it he would need it awful bad.

Satisfied, he shoved it under his pillow and lay down for a nap. He needed plenty of sleep before he played cards. And the other game he was playing demanded extreme care and the most intense concentration. Life would not give him another chance if he were to let something slip through the carelessness brought on by fatigue.

He forced himself to sleep. He woke up twice;

whenever he turned onto his right side, the pain of Cameron's bullet sear across his right side woke him up with a groan. But when he thought of the scattered mess of bones out there on the high desert, he smiled in contentment and fell asleep immediately.

He awoke at nine. He washed, shaved, strapped on his gun belt and after a quick supper of turkey and apple pie, he walked into the Texas Star.

"Mr. Sheridan! A pleasure to see you back! Won't you join us?" It was Morgan. Slocum smiled and sat down, ordered a drink, and bought himself $200 worth of chips.

There were two strange faces at the table. Morgan introduced them.

"Mr. Hogan. Mr. Byron. Mr. Sheridan."

The three men nodded politely.

"Mr. Hogan and Mr. Byron are ranchers from down Weatherford way," Morgan said. "They're lookin' over ranch properties."

"We're lookin' for good pasture to take our surplus cattle," Hogan said.

Slocum nodded.

Morgan went on. "And Mr. Sheridan—er——"

"Plays cards," Slocum said calmly.

"*All* the time?" Hogan asked.

Slocum looked him over carefully. Hogan was a stocky man of 40, with jet-black hair, a hard-bitten face and a very good suit of black broadcloth. Business must have been good, Slocum decided. Across the man's stomach swung a heavy gold watch chain. As Slocum watched, Hogan dipped a fat thumb and forefinger into his vest pocket, pulled out a gold hunting case and popped it open. He grunted and thrust it back again. Slocum thought the gesture was done somewhat ostentatiously, as if the man wished to call attention to his expensive watch.

"Plays cards all the time, eh?" Hogan repeated. He

turned to Fred Byron and said with a faint sneer, "Hear that, Fred? Mr. Sheridan here plays cards *all* the time." Slocum felt a red tide slowly beginning to rise within him. He knew the danger signs, and he was very well aware that he would have to control himself.

"Not *all* the time, Mr. Hogan. I take time out to sleep."

Slocum noticed that Hogan had reddened blood vessels in his eyes. The man had been drinking. Slocum looked him over carefully. If he had been drinking when he said that, that set up a different equation. But like most drunks, Hogan suddenly shifted to another topic without preliminaries.

"We come up on that goddamn train yestiddy. I ain't never been on such a slow train in my whole goddamn life."

"Yeah," said Slocum, "but look how long you get to ride for a dollar." He lit a cigar. He saw Morgan grinning.

Fred Byron placed his cigar carefully on the ashtray. His hands were well-kept, almost white. Slocum noticed that. He must have spent his life wearing gloves to keep them in that condition. Morgan's hands, on the contrary, were tanned, calloused, scarred, and three of his knuckles had been broken and badly reset while handling cattle. Byron was also well-dressed but there were fresh gravy stains on his gray trousers. The trousers came from a very expensive manufacturer in San Francisco. Both men must have struck it rich in the cattle business.

Byron weighed about 190, Slocum judged. His jaw jutted out like half a brick. His lips were squeezed together as if they had been jammed together with a powerful pair of pliers, so that a tiny knot of muscle showed at each end of his mouth. His brown eyes glittered under his heavy eyebrows. He never seemed to blink. It was the same kind of unwinking stare that Slocum had noticed in snakes. His long sideburns were evened off next to his prominent cheekbones. His hair was thick and chestnut-colored. His shoulders were massive. He moved deliberately, like a man who had a good opinion of himself. It would be an opinion that Slocum might share. Byron would be an ugly customer. Slocum planned to keep a safe distance between them.

"Got any other source of income, Mr. Sheridan?" Hogan asked.

Morgan took a deep breath. He regretted introducing them and he regretted being there. Slocum stared impassively at Hogan. There was something he couldn't quite figure out about them. Slocum had met many drunken and wealthy ranchers in his time, but there was something about the two of them which didn't ring true.

Byron was sober. He saw the green eyes narrow and widen. He knew Slocum was getting ready to handle Hogan—either with a slap across the face, a pistol-whipping across his skull or, if it would go further, a shot.

Byron grabbed Hogan's elbow. "Ed, c'mon. It's time we got some sleep. C'mon!"

Hogan shook him off. "Don' feel sleepy," he said thickly. "Feel like stayin' an' gamblin' an' puttin' this here cheap piker out o' business. I'm a big, bad gamblin' man from Texas, an' I mean to make damn sure there's only four aces in this deck." He leaned towards Slocum and said, "Unnerstan'?"

Slocum relaxed. There would be no satisfaction in tangling with a stupid drunk. And his friend seemed to be able to handle him. There would be no satisfaction in being forced to shoot. And that was where Slocum would be heading for if he stayed in the saloon. But his policy was to keep his head down low and not attract attention from the sheriff until he'd be good and ready. And he was not ready. He had too many things to handle, including a projected private meeting with Mrs. Hamilton.

Slocum stood up, nodded to Morgan, said, "Good evenin', sir," and was on his way out before Hogan realized what was happening.

Slocum didn't feel like playing anywhere else that night. He felt angry, tense and disturbed by the two strangers. He walked slowly to the edge of town, turned around and walked back, smoking a cigar with his hands plunged into his pockets.

He passed by the sheriff's house. He heard a piano being played. His mother used to play, and play well. He stopped to listen, leaning against a tree. She was playing Schubert. She played adequately enough. He could see into the drawing room. He could make out her hands in the soft glare of the lamp bracketed to the wall, which she had had covered with some elaborately flowered design. In Slocum's old house there was nothing but well-oiled walnut paneling.

He could see her hands flashing back and forth over the keyboard, and the thin gold band on her left hand. In an armchair beyond the piano sat Hamilton.

Slocum pulled on the cigar. Its end suddenly glowed in the darkness under the tree and Mrs. Hamilton saw it. She got up and walked to the window and reached out a white hand for the curtain, looking out curiously. Slocum stepped out boldly from under the shadow of the tree and bowed. She was startled, and in a second the white curtain flashed across the window. Slocum grinned. He went on to his hotel and up to bed.

22

Next morning Slocum went riding. Someone called his name from a hitching rack. It was Morgan, who had just set a foot in a stirrup. Slocum reined in and waited. Morgan mounted and came up alongside.

"Glad I ran 'cross you, Mr. Sheridan. Like to talk a bit."

"Sure."

Morgan rode deep, three or four vertebrae sunk below the cantle.

"I want to 'pologize for them two fellers last night."

"Nothin' to do with you, Mr. Morgan. No need."

"Oh, yes. They ain't friends of mine, but I'm sorta responsible for 'em bein' in Socorro. So I want to thank you for not goin' to war."

Slocum was still simmering about it, but he decided to drop the whole subject.

"It's all over, Mr. Morgan. You got no call to get upset."

"I'm ridin' over to the stockyards, Mr. Sheridan. A couple hundred head comin' in later. If you got no objections, mind if I ride along?"

"No, sir."

Morgan rolled a cigarette and lit it. He shook out the match.

"I played cards long enough with you to get to know you a little," he said. "You want to know a man, jus' play poker with 'im a few weeks. So I know you c'n keep your mouth shut if you're asked. I'm askin'."

"Sure."

"They ain't ranchers."

"I know."

"Well, I'll be diddle dog damned! How'd you figger that out?"

"I'll tell you. Their clothes looked too damn new, for a start. Ranchers don't buy new clothes when they come to look at ranches. An' when two ranchers go 'n' wear brand-new clothes at the same time, an' both with bran' new boots? An' there's somethin' 'bout the way they carry themselves an' the way the bigger one talks. Any rancher talk that way to his men, they'd all be sackin' their saddles an' hittin' the rattler in five minutes. They don't hold for that kind o' talk. They're not ranchers, is all, Mr. Morgan."

Morgan rode along in silence. His sloppily made cigarette was fraying at the end like a rope coming apart. He struck another match and looked sharply at Slocum through the pointed yellow burst of flame till he burned his fingers. He cursed and lit another match.

"Mr. Sheridan, I tell you, if you ever want a job ramroddin' it's yours."

If there was anything that Slocum didn't want to do for a long time, it was being a foreman on a big ranch for a man he liked: The temptation to disappear with a few thousand head would be too strong to resist and the resultant guilt about taking advantage of a friend would be just as strong. And as long as he was wanted for rustling in Montana, it wouldn't hurt to disabuse Morgan.

"Thank you kindly, but I don't know a damn thing 'bout the cow business."

Morgan cocked a skeptical eye but decided it would be best to accept Slocum's statement.

"Well," he said, "Hogan an' Byron are all right. I hired 'em four years ago when they was detectives from the Cattlemen's Association of Arizona. They cleaned up a smart gang of rustlers workin' out of Mescalero who was robbin' me blind. They grabbed on 'em right in the sagebrush flats, caught 'em with runnin' irons. I had a chuck wagon right near, an' a buckboard jus' come up from Tularosa with supplies. They lifted the wagon tongues an' tied 'em together, an' tied the wagons together by the front wheels to keep 'em from rollin' back. They hung both men from the tops of the wagon tongues an' kept 'em hangin' there for three days as a warnin'. When I come by on the fourth day I coulda swore their necks was three feet long. Saved the county the expense of a trial. So I recommended 'em to the Dirty Dog people. You got no idea how they was carryin' on, wantin' people strung up left an' right. So when I tole 'em 'bout Hogan an' Byron an' those four fellers they hung from the wagon tongues up at Mescalero, why, they jumped up an' clicked their heels.

" 'Nother thing Byron handled pretty good. That Byron feller once worked for the Lazy T. He had to ship eighty carloads of hosses down to Mexico for the Mex army. The freight on that was s'posed to be a hunnerd eighty-five a car. So what did Byron do? Why, he jus' studied the rate book. I c'n tell you that was a pretty disgusted agent. Byron found out that horses used for herdin' could be shipped at the same rate as cattle, plus ten dollars a car. So he bought three carloads of calves at eighteen dollars a head. Then he claimed the eighty-dollar-a-car rate, instead of the hunnerd eighty-five.

"He was shippin' one car of calves on each trainload, y' see, Sheridan, explainin' to the agent the hosses were for herdin' purposes. The railroad wanted to know why it took two thousand head of hosses to herd a hunnerd twenty calves, and Byron told him the calves was pretty damn wild! The agent got so rattled he let Byron get away with it. I'm tellin' yuh, Sheridan, the big feller's not only tough, he's damn smart."

"What about the five-thousand-dollar reward?"

"Hell, they'll pay that to any ole bystander who might catch this Slocum feller, but I know for damn sure the Dirty Dog is payin' them pretty good to dig up Slocum, and an extra bonus for the body. They don' care how the body gets dead, either. They're good men, but Hogan can't hold his liquor good. I certainly do appreciate your keepin' your temper. They're workin' for Pinkerton now."

"So they're down here because of the stagecoach robbery?"

"Yep. They already roughed up the two guards. Said they lined up the job for Slocum. Ain't much justice when they show up, but they sure get results. You'll see, if you're here long enough."

"They havin' any luck?"

"They don't tell me. Hogan was once cleaned out by a gambler down to Tucson who used marked cards. He jus' can't forget it. So I'm askin' you to . . . well . . . if you——"

Morgan sought, embarrassed, for the correct words. Slocum supplied them.

"To let 'im paw an' beller an' get out of the road?"

"It's a lot to ask, Sheridan. But they're good men an' know their business. I thought the sheriff could use a little expert help."

"He's not doin' well?"

Morgan spat.

"I'll tell you somethin'. He worked for me once, ten years ago, time when I was livin' out at the ranch, mebbe fifty miles southwest in the flat valley land San Augstin way. He rode into Socorro one day, ridin' one of my ponies. He got drunk. Someone told me he saw my horse tied to a rack outside a saloon. It was October. Said the horse like to died of cold an' hunger. When he came ridin' back three days later, I jerked 'im offen the pony an' put 'im afoot, an' without his consent, an' with his saddle. He lugged it back to town, all the way. That's when he decided to be a cowboy no more. He became a deppity, then got hisself elected. He talks good an' *looks* like a sheriff. So he feels I'm responsible for improvin' his lot in life, y' see?

"You know 'bout that farm boy who saw his first train? He was walkin' along the track, wonderin' what the dang thing was for. Then the train come along. The boy bust out in a dead run, an' jus' stayed between them two rails till he come to the next town, seventeen an' one-half miles away. Someone asked him why he jus' din't step off the track.

" 'If I woulda got over in the plowed ground,' he said, breathin' a little heavy, 'it woulda caught me sure.' Well, Hamilton reminds me of that farm boy. He fooled that pretty wife o' his with his looks an' that sweet talk; but she's sure caught on by now. Well, Sheridan, what say?"

"Mr. Morgan, I'll stay out of their way, is all I c'n promise. Hogan wants to grab himself some fun by pullin' out some o' my tail feathers. I ain't standin' still for that. I ain't gonna look for trouble, an' I ain't gonna give out free tickets for him to walk over me. But I won't go off in his face. I'll have a slow fuse."

"Man can't ask for more. I thank ye kindly."

"How'd you get Hogan to his hotel?"

Morgan grinned. "You'd be surprised what a cup of hot coffee poured down the neck of your shirt c'n do."

23

Slocum liked this time of day very much. It was very quiet inside the saloon. The only sounds were the clink of chips, the soft hiss of cards as they were dealt out and the occasional clunk of a bottle against the big mirror back of the bar as the bartender returned it to the glass shelf. The street was fiery hot. Some cowboys were amusing themselves by writing special-delivery letters every half hour to an old laundress who lived on the far side of Socorro. The irate post-master had to keep his horse saddled constantly for instant action. Each time he mounted his horse with another special-delivery letter the cowboys howled with laughter.

The swinging doors of the saloon suddenly opened. They stayed open.

Slocum looked up curiously. A large man was silhouetted against the blinding glare of the street. The man stood till his eyes had become adjusted to the dim light of the interior. Then he moved. The doors swung in and out, then creaked to a halt. It was Hamilton. He saw Slocum and moved to his table.

Hamilton was a tall, heavy redhead, slowly going to fat. His hair was naturally curly, but it had a kind of flatness to its color, like a brick covered with dust. It nowhere approached his wife's brilliant glowing luster. He was ruddy, with a face that was florid and that would, in a few years, be covered with broken veins if he did not watch his drinking. He wore black serge trousers, custom-tailored, like a wealthy rancher, custom-tailored black serge coats and white linen shirts. He never bothered with ties, a source of mild friction with Mrs. Hamilton. A gold watch chain swung across his big chest. In the vest pocket nestled an expensive Swiss gold watch with a locomotive engraved on the lid. It chimed the half hours and hours. He wore expensive black boots. He wore the sheriff's star over his left breast pocket. He was doing well, everyone could see that.

He usually wore a relaxed, almost benevolent air which had a great appeal to voters. Women always urged their husbands to vote for him. He gave people the feeling that he was always on top of every situation. He was never flustered. He had been elected three times in a row.

He was in the barbershop every day, talking politics and being shaved. He always looked well groomed. He always told everyone that he had once been a cowpuncher like many of them but that he had quit because he always seemed to wind up on the dusty side of the herds. This amused them and gave them the feeling that he was honest and could be trusted. Hardly anyone knew that he was running a phony vigilante outfit and extorting money from the saloons. Most people assumed that his fine living came from his wife's money. She just plain *looked*, people thought, like she came from a real rich family back east.

He was not a specially evil person. He had a smile for everybody who had a vote. It could be seen by the way that he carried himself that he fancied Mr. Hamilton as a very special kind of person. He was sure that he deserved far more money than he was making, even with the vigilante graft. If Hamilton kept his nose clean, Morgan told Slocum, he stood a good chance winding up one day as the governor.

He had a commanding presence, and this is what had appealed to his wife. He seemed virile, after the usual eastern man who had wooed her, and he seemed to be going somewhere in life—somewhere much more interesting than a dull legal office. So she took a chance and married him, thinking she would be able to educate him in the amenities and subtleties of society. But he was moving too slowly, and she was beginning to simmer with unrest and boredom and resentment.

He moved closer to Slocum and spoke.

"Mornin', Mr. Sheridan," he said, smiling. Slocum did not feel the smile was meant to be friendly. "Been away?"

"Family business." It took effort, but Slocum forced an agreeable tone into his voice.

"Care to step to the bar?"

"Do you mind, sir?" Slocum asked the cowpuncher.

The cowpuncher waved him on.

At the bar Slocum said, "What'll you have, Sheriff?"

Hamilton took out two silver dollars and slid them down the bar. "I'm decoratin' the mahogany," he said.

Slocum sipped his drink. Hamilton gulped his down. "Mighty hot out there," he said feelingly.

"Sure is," Slocum said. He waited patiently for what the sheriff had to say.

Hamilton pushed his glass around in circles on the damp bar.

"Been away?"

"Yes."

"Hot in Chicago, eh?"

"Sure is." And how word gets around, Slocum thought. He sipped and waited. Hamilton frowned at his drink. He was edging nervously towards his purpose, Slocum knew, and he breathed a sigh of secret relief. He didn't get the feel that Hamilton had him connected with the bullion robbery.

A cowboy with whom Slocum had played a dozen or so hands that morning, lifted his head from his arms. "Hey, le's play some more cards! I come here ever' two months to git me some Meskin tail an' play me a good game! Where's game?"

"Go home," the sheriff said with an air of bored menace.

"Ain't got a home," the cowboy said mournfully.

"Go to your hotel!" Hamilton said sharply.

"Ain't got a hotel. Registered f'r a night's lodgin' in a haystack. More money f'r poker. Le's get goin', folks!"

"We can't talk here," Hamilton said angrily. "S'pose you drop over my house 'round ten. 'Round the alley side."

Slocum nodded. Hamilton left. So he wanted Slocum after dark? By the back entrance? He had something dirty up his sleeve, Slocum thought as he walked back to the green baize table.

" 'At sheriff reminds me o' Lincoln," the cowboy said, " 'cause he's so diff'runt." He laughed convulsively at his own joke. Then he began to build up his chips in little piles and ended up knocking them over with a dirty forefinger. "Hey," he demanded, "ever git fired ninety miles from a railroad? Jus' happened to me. I traded a steer for a jar o' brandied cherries, an' the boss found out. Now, you lissen, mister," he went on angrily, "you wanna play cards or you wanna fart 'round with the sheriff? You're s'posed to gamble an' nothin' else! You——" He twisted sideward and threw up onto the sawdust-covered floor.

Slocum backed away. He did not find card-playing exciting. He didn't like the smoke-filled air and the sudden joviality of men released from months of long, hard, lonely work on the trail or the range; men who had one night to blow steam and who were determined to make up for three months of sweat and bad food in one night.

Slocum lit a cigar and drew on it carefully until the end glowed perfectly. He turned around and looked at the cowboy. The man was feeling better. The broken-down old cowpuncher with a badly healed smashed pelvis who swept out the saloon and emptied the cuspidors had cleaned up the mess under the table.

"How 'bout 'nother hand, gamblin' man?"

Slocum didn't like the man's tone. By ten o'clock he had won the cowboy's wages for three months of line riding.

24

It was evening now and Slocum was in pain. Whenever the weather was cold and damp his shoulder began to ache. And now a chilly mist had drifted up from the river and was sliding its wet tendrils in and out of the streets of Socorro.

Slocum rode slowly. Idly he counted more than 30 ponies tied to hitching racks in front of the Texas Star. The saloon was so packed with people that he could hardly see the bar. Some drunken cowboy had let out a yell and fired five gunshots out of sheer high spirits. A lamp on the piano was smoking badly and giving a little light, its smashed chimney strewn over the top of the piano. No one seemed to be paying any attention. The piano player was still working calmly. Two cowboys walked unsteadily out of the saloon and mounted their ponies.

"I told ya not to shoot, you dumb bastard," one said conversationally. "That bartender's got a mighty fast draw with that ole pick handle."

Slocum noticed that the man he was talking to was holding a bandanna to the side of his head. It was sopping wet with blood.

"Aw, so what?" the cowpuncher said calmly. "He was a little bit fussy, wa'n't he? See that mirror back of the bar? That cost more'n a hunnerd-sixty-acre farm. Next time we come I'm gonna bust it with three shots. Three."

"I ain't gonna be with yuh, you c'n count on *that.*"

He paid no attention. "Three shots. Three. One in the top, one in the middle an' one smack on the bottom. I bet it'll crack open just as nice. Wanna bet?"

"I ain't bettin' you anythin', you crazy Arkansas bastard."

"I'm savin' that mirror for the next time we come in from line ridin'. You wait, Phil."

"S'pose someone else busts it first?"

"I'll kill 'im, hombre. I'll kill 'im."

Slocum grinned. Typical line riders' conversation and actions, he thought. He had been like that once.

By the time he reached the sheriff's house his shoulder was worse than ever, and he was full of hate for the man who had broken it.

The sheriff was waiting in the alley back of his house.

Slocum dismounted. Neither spoke. Hamilton led the horse into the stable. It was a big one, big enough to hold Mrs. Hamilton's sulky at the far end. Bales of hay were stacked up above. Two fine saddle horses stopped munching their oats to look at Slocum, their ears pricked forward. Well-oiled harness and two fine saddles hung from oak pegs sunk into two upright beams. Slocum recognized the saddles as coming from the best saddle man in Houston. They were very expensive, not the kind of thing you'd expect to see owned by a sheriff in a small New Mexican town. It was clear that Hamilton took in a lot of money—and it was just as clear that he was spending just about all of it.

"Come on in, Sheridan. The missus made a pot of coffee."

The kitchen was big and comfortable, with blue curtains at the windows and roses in a copper bowl on the window ledge. A blue enameled coffeepot simmered on the stove. Two mugs were on the table. A kerosene lamp with a green glass shade stood in the center of the round oak table. Beside each mug was a white cloth napkin and neatly centered on each napkin was a coffee spoon.

"Wife likes things high-class," Hamilton said proudly.

Slocum sat down. Hamilton poured out the coffee.

"Sheridan," he said, "here's the deal. Cameron used to work for me. I been waitin' for him to show up, an' I'm gettin' awful tired waitin'. He used to take off three, four days at a time without a word to me or anyone, but now it's been a month an' my business can't wait. He likes to go down Sonora way. Likes them Mex gals. He's got a shaft like a horse an' it rattles when he trots."

Not anymore, Slocum thought.

"Want to do his job? It pays good."

"Doin' what?"

The sheriff poured condensed milk into his coffee. He stirred in sugar. He took a sip. He put in more sugar. He sipped again. Slocum knew the man was weighing his decision again on whether to confide in him.

Slocum sat waiting calmly, sipping the coffee. He watched the sheriff push his saucer back and forth. The night was very quiet. A dog barked in the next yard. A horseman went by with a medley of sounds: hooves clopping in the dust, leather creaking, a jingle of bit and bridle.

Hamilton disappeared briefly and came back with a bottle and two glasses. He filled them and began drinking his right away.

He put down his emptied glass. "Cameron collected for me," he said, his voice stronger and assured. "Y'unnerstan'?"

Slocum shook his head, pretending ignorance.

"Cameron organized the vigilantes 'round here. There was some rustlin', some horse-stealin', there was some 'pache raids. Sometimes some Mex'cans over to Magdalena would go 'n' shoot up a cowboy bar. Some of the sheriffs or town marshals wa'n't much good. An' the U.S. marshals got too much ground to cover. So he organized 'em—I sort o' gave 'im the idea—it wasn't hard. But there wasn't no money in it. So I gave 'im the idee of protectin' each saloon from bein' shot up."

"Or bein' raided by 'paches," Slocum said drily.

The sheriff chuckled. "Trouble was, no one was shootin' up no saloons in Socorro. But, hell, I figger you know how they could get themselves right sudden needin' protection. We worked out two dollars a day f'r each table, see? An' if they di'n't want to pay, why, somehow or other, a fight would start, an' the way two or three cowboys will bust up them expensive mirrors back of the bar is somethin' awful. They got to send all the way to San Francisco for new ones."

Hamilton grinned. "So," he went on, with a satisfied grin, "they coughed up their two dollars. It brought in a lot. I got two-thirds."

"Suppose he held back some?"

Hamilton poured out another glass.

"Oh, no. *No.* I knew too much 'bout that rascal's buggerin' 'round. I could send him up to the Territorial Prison and get 'im to sewin' burlap bags for ten to fifteen any time, an' he goddamn well knew it." Hamilton's grin was wider.

"Yeah."

"Well, looks like he's gone now. Never stayed away this long. Mebbe he shot off his mouth too much to the wrong man. Mebbe it was a case of slow. Nemmind. I know you c'n use some extra money. An' I figger you c'n keep your mouth shut."

Slocum thought that if Hamilton only had some secret and damaging information about him he'd be as happy as a pig in shit. It would make the man relax. It would be nice, Slocum thought with amusement, to help the sheriff relax. Perhaps some small nugget of dirty past behavior on his part?

Slocum decided to provide something in that line.

"Your shoulder hurtin'?"

That was bad. Slocum had been rubbing it absentmindedly. He would have to remember not to do it except when he was alone. The sheriff's remark made him realize he was facing a minor problem. Sooner or later the sheriff would see or find out about his shoulder. The two scars were very obviously entrance and exit wounds. They had very clearly been made by a rifle or carbine bullet. And the posse had been firing Winchesters at him. He might be able to make the connection. Slocum needed a good story right away that would sound very convincing.

"Yeah." Slocum shook his head ruefully. "Someone shot me once, down in Old Mexico. When we were crossin' the river into Arizona." He hesitated, then in a surge of seeming confidence which he knew Hamilton would like, he added, "We had 'bout two hundred head with us. Bought 'em cheap."

"Yeah. Bought 'em at night!"

Slocum winked. As he had guessed, the sheriff liked his confession of criminal behavior. It gave him the kind of grip he was looking for.

"Where'd it happen?" asked Hamilton, with an air of extreme casualness.

"Oh, near Papago Wells," Slocum said easily. Hamilton's face expressed a look of bland unconcern. He was overdoing it, Slocum thought. He added, "Sure, I'd like to pick up some extra money. I certainly can use it."

"All right. You jus' go 'round 'n' tell everyone you're pickin' up instead of Cameron. Any trouble, you tell me. Is it a deal?"

"Deal."

They shook hands. As soon as he felt the sheriff's touch, Slocum had an impulse to jerk him forward and smash his barrel across Hamilton's nose, spoiling his good looks. For a start. Then he would have liked . . . he called a halt to his fantasies.

"Le's—le's celebrate," Hamilton said. His speech

was slurred. He poured out his glass to the brim once again. Slocum's glass only needed an inch of whiskey. He sipped his. Hamilton tossed his off as if it were water.

"You hang out in the saloons," he said. "You—you jus' keep your eyes open. Ri'? You seen them two men claimin' they're ranchers buyin' property?"

Slocum nodded.

"Well, they ain't. They're detectives. They're—they come up here tryin' to find a lead into that bullion robb'ry happened a couple weeks after you went to Chicago. They put a story together that Cameron done it. That's 'cause he tole people he was goin' up to the mines for a couple weeks' work recoverin' mercury from the tailin's. I checked it out myself. The mine never heard of 'im. So they figure he did it, got hisself a friend an' mebbe made it down to Mexico or's holed up somewhere in the mountains, in a sheepherder's cabin, somewhere like that, till it blows over."

"You don't think that's what happened?"

"Nope. I know Cameron. He's not smart enough to plan somethin' like that hisself. But he's smart enough to tie in with a smart one. An' then right after, Cameron shot 'im. Plumb in the back. Then he took it all."

"Why couldn't the other man shoot Cameron an' take it all?"

"Mebbe. We telegraphed all 'round the Territory. No one's been anywhere with a load of bullion. They talked to all the banks an' assay people."

Hamilton didn't realize he had shifted his theory about Cameron in a complete about-face. First he was sure that Cameron had gone off on a toot to Mexico. Now he seemed convinced that Cameron had been involved in the robbery. Credit the two men from the Pinkerton Agency for that, Slocum thought. They were smart.

"But them two detectives're stupid."

Sure, Slocum thought. Hamilton would have to prove to himself that there had to be something wrong with them—after all, they had proved to him that he was completely wrong about Cameron.

"Wanna know why?" Hamilton demanded.

"Sure."

"Instead of talkin' to sheriffs on both sides of the border, they keep hangin' 'round here in Socorro."

Slocum listened intently.

"Why?"

"Why?" Hamilton repeated, pouring more whiskey. "I'll tell you why. 'Cause they say Cameron did it with a friend. An' they say the friend is here, right here in Socorro. They say it was done real smart. An' a real smart man wouldn't try to move 'round with two tons of gold. He'd hide it somewhere an' feed it into a bank or an assay office a little at a time. An' the best way to handle it, they say, is for the man to stay where he lives, so's no one would get nosy. So they're here tryin' to dig up his friend."

Slocum didn't like the sound of that at all. But he said calmly and judiciously, "Sounds smart, all right."

"Sounds stupid! Nobody here liked Cameron. He was a no-good dirty sonofabitch. If he ain't in hell right now there ain't nobody there. I'm tellin' you, someone real smart hooked on to him, planned it an' killed 'im. An' they're wastin' time lookin' for a *friend* of 'is. Goddamn fools. They don' want no advice from me an' they sure ain't gonna get none, sure as God made Sundays.

"But I'd sure like to latch on to that two tons of bullion, I sure would. I used to work once on a gold strike up Idaho ways. Good clean Snake River dust used to fetch eighteen dollars an ounce. Most times you'd find a trace in each pan an' you'd be lucky to get two bits out of it. You'd break your back shovelin' an' swishin' that gravel 'round an' your hands would freeze in that mountain water. Sometimes I'd work a week, seven days, fourteen hours a day, an' make ten dollars. Goddamn, *two million* bucks all at once!"

He heaved a deep, envious sigh.

"So, Sheridan, you hang 'round, play poker an' see what you c'n pick up from the Pinks. They ain't talkin' to me much, an' I sure ain't gonna talk to *them*. But I sure like to know what's on their minds. What say? Besides collectin' the taxes?"

Why not? Slocum thought. If he didn't need the money, what was that story about him going to Chicago and telling Tompkins and Morgan about his money problems? And if he didn't need the money, had he lied about the purpose of his trip to Chicago? And if he had, then why?

Too dangerous to refuse. Hamilton might very well decide that there was something fishy about him. Slocum didn't want anyone to get the idea that he was nothing else than a gambler who desperately needed some extra money.

He was locked into that format. The pattern of his constant need for money had to be maintained. That was the only thing that could save him from the relentless curiosity of the Pinkerton men.

And he knew why the sheriff wanted to hear what the two Pinks said. If they found a good lead to the bullion—and happened to let it drop in some drunken talk—the sheriff would gladly yield both his balls to be there first, Slocum was sure. And guess how much gold would get itself returned to the Dirty Dog!

"Sure," Slocum said, "glad to do it."

He concealed his pleasure. He liked the idea that Hamilton would be feeding him anything he knew about the Pinkertons. And he liked the thought that Hamilton had a strong passion to put his hands on a large amount of bullion.

It was a dangerous passion. Like all great sources of energy, it had to be directed or it would backfire. Once, years before, Slocum went partners in Nevada with a man to go placer mining in a stream running through a valley before it made its junction with the Carson River west of Dayton. They had rustled together once and had gotten along. He liked Owen.

On the third day they came across a tiny pocket in the rocky stream bed. They pried out a dozen pea-sized nuggets. Slocum put them all in a small glass jar and handed it to Owen. Owen, new to placer mining, hefted it, surprised at the weight. Slocum bent down to get a pickax, and when he straightened up Owen was still staring at the gold in the glass jar.

Slocum was not easily frightened, but he never had forgotten Owen's face. It was flooded with great excitement. The man was actually panting. Slocum packed up immediately, took his half and rode off within 15 minutes. He knew he could never feel relaxed around Owen anymore.

But it was just this lust that would make Hamilton edge himself deeper into the web Slocum had to spin for him. Oh, Slocum thought, with a tight smile, it was a very useful lust.

25

Slocum wrote a postcard once a week to his imaginary sister in Chicago. They were all addressed to Mrs. Martha Nortner, 5350 Kildee Street. They never got there. There was no such person or street, and since there was no return address, they would wind up in the dead-letter office out in Chicago and never go farther.

On the other hand Slocum would receive a card from the imaginary lady every so often. It would read like this—or a variation thereof: "Dear Brother Sam: It was very good to hear from you. I am glad you are all rite. The children miss you. We like the new house and wish you wood visit us agen soon. Yours very sinceerly, your loving sister Martha."

This deception was accomplished by his writing a letter to an ex-rustler friend living in Chicago. The letter contained the text of the card Slocum wanted written to him. Pete wrote out the text in his handwriting and mailed the card.

There was no way the cards could be traced. And every postmaster in every small town, as Slocum knew well, would read every postcard if business was slow. And business was slow in Socorro.

Sooner or later, Slocum knew, someone would check on his Chicago story. This bit of deception would come in useful.

Slocum bumped into Joe Riley, one of Hamilton's deputies, just outside the post office. The post office was a small clapboard shack next to the livery stable where Slocum kept his horse. The usual flag hung in a dispirited fashion from a short flagstaff crudely nailed above the door. The flag had not been taken in ever since it had been placed there three years before. The fierce New Mexican summer sun had bleached it uniformly till the red bars and forty-six stars were almost as pale as the white elements in the field. The silk was badly frayed at the edges from flapping itself to death in the sudden bitterly cold northers which swept down the valley from time to time. Since it was not Slocum's flag he felt no indignation over this state of affairs, although there were aroused citizens' complaints from time to time made to the postmaster. This gentleman invited everyone—except the ladies—to go kiss his ass or write to the Postmaster General, whichever they preferred. So far neither suggestion had ever been acted upon.

Once inside the door, there was a bulletin board. This was simply the north wall. On it were tacked all the official proclamations, homesteading laws, mining regulations, postal fees and several interesting *Wanted* posters. Slocum always cocked an amused eye at his whenever he entered. Since he had entered the penitentiary under an assumed name, Richard Hart McCann, his photograph was filed under that name and no warden had ever made the connection between McCann and Slocum. Therefore, the posters only exhibited whatever fancy struck the police artist after listening to nervous eyewitnesses describe Slocum. The result was that a snarling monster glared out from the post office wall. Slocum liked to stop in front of it and light his cigar, enjoying the work of the imaginative artist.

"Mornin', Sheridan," Riley said, with some sourness. Riley was holding some official letters he was about to mail. Riley had wanted to be appointed Hamilton's collector and he was angry that the job had gone to Slocum.

"Mornin', Riley," Slocum said politely. Riley gambled occasionally.

Riley put down the letters and bought seven stamps.

He tore off the first stamp, licked it, put it deliberately off center on the envelope and slammed his fist down on the stamp as hard as he could.

The postmaster looked up, startled.

"Goddamnit almighty, Joe, what the hell's the matter with you?"

"Goddamn sheriff treats me like an errand boy," Riley muttered.

"Well, godalmighty, don't go 'round bustin' up guvvamint property!"

All this conversation gave Slocum time to read the

address on the first envelope. It read, "Sheriff, Papago Wells, Arizona." He read it with great interest. Papago Wells was where he had told Hamilton he had brought some rustled cattle across the river from Mexico.

Slocum walked out of the post office, suppressing a smile. So Hamilton was checking up on him! It showed he had an admirable instinct for playing it carefully before he committed himself more deeply. Oh, Slocum thought, good!

The next two weeks went by peaceably. The saloonkeepers acknowledged Slocum as the collector for Hamilton. Frank Osborn sourly pointed out that the sheriff had plenty of expenses lately.

"He's arrestin' lots of men who oughtn't be arrested," he said, "but there are mileage fees to consider."

Almost everywhere he went Slocum was getting hints and flat-out statements that Hamilton liked money, wanted it and would do plenty to get it.

On Monday nights Slocum rode to Hamilton's house. Always very late, and always to the back door, as Hamilton had requested. Slocum handed over the money. Hamilton would count it and hand him his share.

"Can't let you in," he said somewhat embarrassed. "The wife's sure you got me drunk that night, an' she wants me to keep away from you, Sheridan."

"Sure."

"You know how women are."

I sure do, Slocum thought. So that's what she tells him. She doesn't want me near her at all.

The sheriff went back inside with the bills jammed inside his pants pocket. The door closed and the bolt rammed shut.

Slocum stood outside the door. He took out a cigar and walked slowly to his horse. He lit the cigar and shook out the match, staring at the house. You bet, he thought grimly, you *bet* I'm a bad influence.

26

Slocum's luck at poker and faro was good for the next few days. He decided to go to Albuquerque and buy some new clothes and to drop in and see Barrett. Barrett had a keen nose for news of deep interest to people like Slocum. Besides, nothing much could be done with Hamilton until he got his mail back from Papago Wells. So Slocum went to Albuquerque.

He bought a flowered silk vest as befitted a successful gambler. He bought three more white shirts and a pair of new boots. He dropped in Barrett's office.

The gray-bearded assayer smiled broadly when he saw Slocum. He was ten years older than Slocum and whenever they saw each other, even though years might have passed, he smiled with an air of quiet affection which touched the younger man. Barrett never mentioned what Slocum had done for him during the war but it was clear that the man's gratitude showed in his smile.

The windowsills were covered with ore samples. Two long tables held more specimens. One glittering rock sat by itself on a small table next to the door where anyone entering was bound to see it as soon as he entered. A cardboard sign was propped against the rock. It read:

THIS IS IRON PYRITE. IT IS COMMONLY CALLED FOOL'S GOLD. IF YOUR SPECIMEN LOOKS JUST LIKE THIS, THE NAME HAS BEEN CORRECTLY CHOSEN. JUST GO AWAY.

Barrett wore a green eyeshade, the kind worn by bookkeepers. He could have been a bookkeeper himself, except that his gray eyes were too sharp. He had made himself a small holster which he wore around his calf. He kept a two-barreled derringer in it. He had used it twice in the six years he had been wearing it. Each time he had pretended to faint when the robber had demanded the contents of his safe. Once the man's attention had been distracted, Barrett had pulled the little gun and fired both barrels at once. He had killed each man instantly. He had not been bothered since the last time, which was two years ago. That green eyeshade, Slocum knew, was very deceptive.

Slocum nodded. The pungent fumes of acid seemed to penetrate every corner of the office. It was perfume to Barrett.

"Couple fellows been around," Barrett said without preamble. He never indulged in polite conversation. Slocum grunted.

"Wanted to know if some fellow had been selling bullion in big amounts. Said he had green eyes and wore white shirts like some fellows do in Texas when they're running for office. *They* said that, not me. Didn't mention your name, or where you were from, but it was you, all right. Told 'em no such person showed up here, but if he did I'd let 'em know. And since they're working for private parties, I played anxious to know how much was in it for me. The dark-haired one said if my testimony held up in court I'd get a thousand bucks. I figured it had to do with the Dirty Dog holdup, and I hinted as much. They turned nasty. I told them I didn't want them hollering in my rain barrel. They kept it up. I hauled out my shotgun from under the bench and they apologized right smart. They said they'd make it two thousand. Then I asked for it in writing." He grinned.

"Then?"

"So the fools put it down. Here."

He pulled out his wallet and extracted a small sheet of paper.

Slocum read it.

"In the event that the man or men who robbed the Dirty Dog stagecoach of bullion are arrested due to the information given by Henry Barrett, assayer, of Albuquerque, we promise to pay him two thousand dollars if they are convicted. Edward Hogan."

Slocum handed it back. "Sounds legal," he said, "but if you try—or anyone tries—to collect, you'll be as busy as a stump-tailed bull in fly-time. The company'll say the offer wasn't made by them, and they're not responsible for the acts of their agents. They won't pay. And if you go huntin' for the Pinks, why, they'll be out of the Territory."

Barrett nodded. Slocum looked sharply at the man's face. They had always gotten on well. Slocum trusted him—perhaps not 100 percent. If the man could be rated on a reliability scale, Slocum would go for 96 percent.

"I heard of someone who tried to collect a reward like that," he said in a friendly manner. "He tried to collect it on someone who trusted him. Named Gibson."

"Gibson?"

"Merle Gibson. Bank robbery. Montana. Gibson went to the territorial prison. Broke rock for fifteen years. Had to serve every day of it. But he had friends on the outside. 'Bout six months later I saw a teamster come into town. He had a gunny sack filled with a human skeleton he found when he was out there pickin' up buffalo bones for fertilizer. They knew who it was right away. The man who did the informin' had a plate on the left side of his head from Second Manassas. The plate was there, all right, and the right side of the skull was blown away by a forty-five bullet someone must have shot from maybe an inch or two away."

Barrett frowned.

Slocum looked at him, his face expressionless.

It never hurt to clear the air with delicate hints. That, Slocum thought, might tend to shift Barrett to 100 percent on his handmade reliability scale.

Slocum sat in the dusty day coach with his long legs thrust into the aisle. He was admiring his new boots. Then he crossed his arms and stared out of the dirty window. The cornfields of the Pueblo Indians slid by on his right. On his left the casual brown current of the Rio Grande flowed strongly to the Gulf of Mexico.

He noticed none of it. He was thinking about the two Pinkerton men. They were not so stupid as he had first thought. Maybe they couldn't hold their liquor, but they were smart.

He cursed silently.

"Socorrrrrro!" yelled the conductor.

27

Slocum's gambling luck continued to be good. So he bought a fine chestnut gelding for $300 and boarded it at Reilly's Livery. He took it out every morning for exercise. One morning he saw Mrs. Hamilton stepping off her front porch as he was riding by. She wore a dress of white muslin, high in the neck and closed at the wrists.

Each of the times he had come to Hamilton's house with the money he was collecting, she had managed to stay out of sight from the time he came to the time he left.

Now he was facing her directly.

He lifted his hat and reined in. She nodded coldly, a pink flush spreading upwards above the white muslin. She looked stunning, Slocum thought, with her masses of coppery-red hair piled into a neat bun at the nape of her neck.

Slocum kept his chestnut at a slow walk beside her as she walked quickly towards Nelson's General Store.

"Nice day, ma'am," he observed genially.

"Yes." She quickened her pace.

"Couldn't be better."

"No."

"Warm, but a nice cool wind off the river."

"Yes." Her heels drummed ever more rapidly along the boardwalk.

"You keep it up, ma'am, you'll be workin' up a real hard sweat."

She said nothing.

"But it would be a pleasure, ma'am, to rub you down."

She flushed even more but did not slacken her pace.

"Missed seein' you at the house, ma'am."

She stopped abruptly. "Yes, Mr. Sheridan. Every time you come I find I have a severe headache." Her teeth were clenched together tightly and the pink flush had deepened to red.

She resumed her walking.

"Good mornin', ma'am," Slocum said politely. He lifted his hat and cantered off.

That night was the regular delivery night. He tied the chestnut to the hitching rack in front of the Texas Star. He pushed through the bat-wing doors and into the saloon.

Business was booming. Railroad men were bellying up to the bar, lined up elbow to elbow with cowpunchers. The piano was tinkling valiantly, and a rouged girl was trying to sing. No one was listening. She had closed her eyes and was singing to herself, swaying in time with the music. She was drunk. Slocum looked at her briefly. He judged that she was good for another three, four years in towns like Socorro before she began to have too many wrinkles. Then she would begin to slide down the scale of cow towns until she would wind up somewhere in North Dakota entertaining half-breeds and teamsters. She would very likely be dead in a cheap cow-town crib within five years. Slocum shrugged to himself, thinking, poor girl. Cigarette smoke turned the air blue. The bartender was working so hard that his shirt was wet with sweat. One cowpuncher was wrestling with a friend on the sawdust-covered floor. People were grinning and giving them plenty of room. One man stood up, reached under the other cowpuncher's shoulders and began to pull him towards the doors.

The cowpuncher on the floor, feeling himself sliding through the sawdust, simply lifted both legs high in the air and drove his spurs into the wooden floor. The rowels locked into the wood fibers. But his friend tightened his grip and continued to pull. He pulled the man right out of his boots, leaving them pinned to the floor.

Slocum smiled as he walked by, watching the bootless cowpuncher walk back in his dirty socks, kneel and wrestle his boots out of the wooden flooring. Suddenly he was aware of the Pinkerton men.

They were leaning against the bar. They looked at him. Hogan whispered into Byron's ear. Byron laughed uproariously, nodded, looked again at Slocum, grinned and bought a bottle of rye from the bartender. Hogan kept pounding his back and laughing. They were still dressed like well-to-do ranchers. Each wore a black serge coat and black serge trousers. Both wore white shirts which cried out for laundering.

Their boots needed a good polish. They looked as if they had been doing some hard traveling, sleeping in their clothes and moving without a sufficient change of shirts or underwear. Both needed shaves and haircuts. They stood laughing and looking at Slocum. Suddenly Hogan dug Byron in the ribs and both men walked out of the saloon.

So much the better, Slocum thought. That avoided the possibility of a clash. He didn't want any trouble to mess up his budding schemes for the Hamilton family.

Five minutes later he noticed people slipping out of the saloon. He could hear titters of laughter coming from the street. From time to time the saloon doors swung open and a grinning face looked in at him and withdrew, and the doors would swing shut again.

Slocum didn't like any of this. But he played on calmly, as if nothing out of the ordinary was happening.

Morgan, as usual, was playing that night with Slocum. The old cowman had noticed the two Pinkerton men's behavior. He didn't like to see them drinking. He had learned that they were not able to hold their liquor well, and he had watched their byplay when Slocum had walked in. He had not liked the fact that several men had slipped outside and were now poking open the doors, grinning at their table and slipping outside again.

"Excuse me a second, Sheridan," Morgan said. He got up and walked out to the street to take a look for himself. He came back almost immediately.

"Better go take a look at your pony," he said with a troubled expression. "Someone's playin' a practical joke that ain't too funny."

Slocum murmured, "Excuse me, gentlemen. I'll be right back." He put down his hand, walked across the saloon and pushed open the doors.

Byron had the whiskey bottle upended above the chestnut's mouth. The last few drops were trickling in. Hogan had untied the reins from the hitching post and was holding them. Byron pulled the empty bottle away from the chestnut's mouth and Hogan dropped the reins.

The chestnut took a few tentative steps, as if to see if his legs were still attached. Then he stuck his nose to the ground and bawled like a cow that had lost her calf. Then he whipped his head back and stood up on his hind legs. He fell over backwards, breaking the saddle horn at its base. He lurched unsteadily to his feet, shook his head violently and leaned heavily against the hitching post for a few seconds. Then he figure-eighted 40 feet across the dusty street and back again, scattering the laughing bystanders.

He plunged straight through the alley that ran six feet wide between the saloon and the general store, bucking, sunfishing and bellowing, working himself like a small tornado among kerosene barrels, empty crates, wheelbarrows and coils of barbed wire.

When he had finally jammed himself between the feed barn and a privy, with his left hind leg stuck inside a wheelbarrow wheel, Slocum was able to catch him. He could control the chestnut only by twisting an ear. Slocum led him out of the alley. The chestnut shuddered and retched as Slocum walked him unsteadily through the mob of grinning faces. The two Pinkerton men were weak from laughter.

The chestnut's legs were badly scratched by the barbed wire. Slocum didn't know whether the tendons were severed or only bruised. The chestnut was limping so badly that only a careful inspection in good light would tell. All the way to the livery stable the horse lurched and staggered. Slocum's rage heated up on the way, as if someone were dumping shovelful after shovelful of coal into his boiler.

He stripped off the saddle and blanket. The horse was sweating profusely. Slocum gave the hostler five dollars and told him to keep the chestnut rubbed down and dry and to send immediately for Doc Eisler, the vet'inary. Then he walked back to the Texas Star, simmering in his fury.

The alley was still a mess. Everyone had gone inside. The two Pinkerton men were at the bar. They tensed as Slocum entered, but he gave no sign that he was aware of their presence as he went by them. Their voices rose triumphantly as Slocum continued to walk towards the table he had left minutes before. He noticed the curious faces of the men at his table. He knew they were wondering why he had said nothing to Hogan and Byron.

"Nice hoss," Byron said loudly, "but can't hold his liquor."

"Yep," Hogan answered, "but he's gonna acquire a taste for it. After t'night, that chestnut is gonna stick his nose into ev'ry trash barrel back of ev'ry saloon in town, lickin' up a drop here an' a drop there."

An amused titter ran through the crowd.

One of Slocum's habits, when he was furious, was to speak very softly and slowly, as if another Slocum were listening. This second Slocum would then, by his calmness, present a good example to the first Slocum, who then would be able to control himself. Slocum knew his rages sometimes shook him till he was helpless in their grip, like a terrier with a rat. He seized upon any help when he sensed one of his cyclonelike rages coming.

"Gentlemen," he said softly, "if you've no objection, I'm cashin' in my chips."

The men looked at him in surprise.

"I might be somewhat busy soon," Slocum said so softly that it was almost a whisper, "an' I'd surely hate to leave the game in a somewhat confused state."

"Sure," Morgan said.

"Thank you all kindly," Slocum said. He picked up his money, folded it and shoved it into his pocket. He turned towards the bar. The men at the table rose and moved towards the far wall.

Morgan saw that the detectives had been drinking heavily. Their natural caution had vanished. Morgan's judgment was that Slocum was a man who would allow himself to be pushed just so far and no further. Moreover, Morgan had noticed that when Slocum was cashing in his chips he had pulled up his Colt and let it slide back easily into its holster. Morgan knew the signs of a professional preparing the tools of his trade.

Slocum walked slowly to the bar. He stood beside the Pinkertons. He ordered a bottle of whiskey. He paid for it. He turned towards Byron.

Without warning Byron jerked his Colt and shot.

Slocum had time to throw himself sideward to the left. The heavy slug went by just above his right shoulder, through the window, across the street and into a four-by-four upright supporting the second floor of the pharmacy. The explosion left powder burns on his coat and shirt. As Slocum ducked to his left, he drew and smashed the barrel down hard on Byron's right wrist. The man's Colt clattered to the floor.

Slocum reached his left arm around the back of Byron, grabbed the fabric of his coat back of the man's left shoulder and spun him around till Byron faced Hogan. Slocum's left arm went around Byron's neck; his right hand jammed the muzzle of his Colt into Byron's right ear. He pulled the hammer back. The click rang out clearly in the suddenly silent saloon.

"Now, sir," he said, almost in a whisper, "this here Colt has a hair trigger. It jus' won't do for anyone to nudge me or start a discussion or even speak loud. Y'unnerstan'?"

Nobody spoke. They saw a man with green eyes and a face that was drained white. Later Morgan was to tell a friend that he would as soon come up against the man as to shove his head into a power saw.

Slocum said into Byron's left ear, "Sir, I asked you if you unnerstood."

"Yeah," Byron croaked.

"Good. Now, if you'll ask your partner here to feed you some whiskey from my bottle there, we c'n get along real nice."

Byron was silent.

Slocum dug the muzzle into Byron's ear with a vicious little circular movement.

"Gimme some whiskey."

"Good. Mr. Hogan?"

Hogan sullenly took the bottle.

"Upend it, please, Mr. Hogan. I do believe you've had some practice lately."

Byron coughed and choked. When he had managed to get half of it down, Slocum urged Hogan to drink the other half. He waited patiently until it was empty.

"Good. Now, gentlemen, you owe me eighteen dollars for a new coat and shirt. Freedman's Haberdashery stocks only the best up in Albuquerque. For repairin' a busted saddle horn, let's say thirty. An' I hope you'll agree when I tell you I'll jus' have to charge you vet fees for my pony. He'll be laid up a week or so, so I know you'll feel it's only fair to pay me some more so's I c'n rent a horse while he's laid up. Let's say a hundred for all of that."

"Ain't got it," Byron growled.

"Borrow it," Slocum said pleasantly.

"Ain't possible."

Slocum twisted the muzzle of the Colt.

"I'll put it up," Morgan said. He pushed through the crowd. He took $210 out of his wallet and handed it to Slocum.

"Thanks," Slocum said. His face, Morgan noticed,

had regained its color. Morgan breathed easier. Slocum added, "Sir, mebbe you'd like to see these gentlemen get home all right. I wouldn't want to see 'em sunfishin' up an' down the alley."

A titter ran through the crowd.

Byron's face flushed red. And Hogan, thoroughly drunk and unable to remain upright without holding on to the edge of the bar, turned his face to look squarely at Slocum in a long, slow, heavy-lidded stare.

Slocum knew from then on the detectives' big aim in life would be to kill him.

It was a pity, Slocum thought. But he did not see what else he could have done.

28

The more Slocum thought about what had just happened the more he was sure he had put his foot in it. There was no way he would be able to live in the same town with those two men.

First, he thought, their professional duties—to find the men who had robbed the Dirty Dog mine—would eventually lead them to him. Sooner or later they would check out his Chicago story. A smart man would look up all wills filed for probate and the obituaries as well. They would go to Chicago to see if they could find a widow who had filed recently whose maiden name was Sheridan.

Maybe they might actually find a widow of that name. But if they went further and looked her up and asked her a few questions they would find out, in ten seconds flat, that a Mr. Samuel Sheridan, presently domiciled in Socorro, Territory of New Mexico, had been lying. And Mr. Sheridan would have quite a sweaty time of it if he would try to explain not only why he had lied, but also where he had been during the Dirty Dog robbery.

Oh, Slocum thought ruefully, they were smart. They couldn't hold their liquor, perhaps, but sober, they were dangerous.

Second, the two Pinkertons now had a personal reason to get him. Sober, they'd be smart enough to behave themselves. Pinkerton headquarters wouldn't stand for their operatives taking up a personal feud whenever it might affect their performance in the field. When they were sober they'd respect their employer's rules. But with a few drinks tucked away they were crazy. Pulling a gun and firing it the way Byron had just done—and risking killing someone who might have been passing by on the street—was not a rational act. Slocum could not deal with people whose behavior was not predictable.

He suddenly had an idea he liked very much.

Slocum had once been in a prison in Cincinnati during the second winter of the war. There was a good library donated by some society women who foolishly thought that if they were to give good books and warm underwear to Johnny Reb, then the South would do the same thing to their Northern prisoners of war. Slocum read all winter, turning the pages with his frostbitten fingers, and he sent the circulation through them again by digging all night with a soup spoon.

By the time spring came he was out of the prison and across the Ohio. But he took with him a residue of the winter's reading. He learned that the Chinese used cormorants for fishing. The birds had a metal ring around their necks and a long leash attached to their legs. They would dive for fish and swallow them, but the metal ring prevented their swallowing the catch completely. The fishermen would haul in the birds and force them to disgorge the fish.

Now, thought Slocum with a thin smile, he would make Hamilton his cormorant. The sheriff would swallow the two Pinkerton men and stop their investigation ice-cold.

Slocum knew how to stop the two detectives from pulling out his tail feathers.

The secret was a four-letter word.

29

The word, of course, was *gold.*

And the time to start was now.

Slocum walked into the livery stable. The vet'inary had come and gone. The chestnut's legs were bandaged. The hostler said that Doc Eisler had said there was nothing seriously wrong, just some bad scratches. They'd heal fine in about ten days. Good, Slocum thought. If a tendon had been severed during that wild pitching down the alley into and out of the coils of barbed wire, he'd have to kill the horse. *Then* he'd have trouble working out his ideas with the Pinkertons. Slocum knew his own furious temper well enough to say a silent prayer of thanks for that.

He lit a cigar and walked slowly towards the sheriff's house. His hands were jammed into his pockets. He thought well when he walked. By the time he had smoked the cigar down to an inch butt, he had it all worked out. He reached the alley that led to the back of the Hamilton house.

He walked down the alley till he reached the back gate. He lifted the latch and pushed the gate. The night was warm and yellow light poured through the open window on the second floor. He walked up the path and before he could knock, he heard angry voices coming from the open window.

"Aw, honey," Hamilton was saying, "what can I do in Frisco? I don't know nobody there."

"You can get a job with the police there, can't you?"

"It ain't that easy."

"Stop saying 'ain't'! I declare, I've told you that *ten thousand* times if I've told you once. How can I take you back east? How can I introduce you to my friends if you can't speak decent English?"

There was a pause. Then Hamilton spoke, trying to control his anger. "I make a pretty good livin', honey."

"Good enough for this abysmal desert town that has one train a day northward to the great and *exciting* city of Albuquerque, and one train a day southbound to the intellectual capital of the west, Las Cruces!" Her voice oozed scorn. "I'm getting awfully, awfully sick of Socorro. There's no one here who likes music, no one who reads anything more than that terrible little newspaper, no one to talk to except the doctor's wife, and from her clothes and conversation I'd say he found her in a bordello."

Slocum grinned. Mrs. Hamilton was right. Mrs. Ripley had come right out of a cow-town crib in Tascosa.

"And," she continued, with a bitter, nagging tone, "I haven't had a chance to wear my new dresses—which *my father* paid for, I'd like to remind you!"

"I thought of movin'," Hamilton said sullenly. "Don't think I didn't. But people jus' don't come into Frisco an' get a job. They got to know someone. An' then they got to start at the bottom."

"Then get to know someone!"

"How? Jus' like that? You think it's easy as pie? You——"

"It doesn't *have* to be San Francisco," she said impatiently. "Don't take me literally. It could be New York. Or Boston. My father knows the mayor of Boston."

"Boston?" asked Hamilton, dismayed. "There's too

many goddamn people stampedin' 'round the streets, some of 'em goin' one way an' some the other. They're all crazy. I don't know if I could stand it."

"Don't you dare curse! I'm not the doctor's wife. I'm a lady. And you'd better learn how to stand it. When I first met you it was all I could do to make you take your hat off whenever you went into a house!"

Slocum turned around and walked quietly to the gate. This time he opened and slammed it shut so that it made plenty of noise. Then he came up the walk, banging his heels hard.

The conversation upstairs stopped before he reached the back door. He knocked.

"Who's there?"

"Sheridan."

"Busy now. Talk to you tomorrow. Ain't it a bit late?"

Her grammar lesson still didn't take, Slocum thought.

"Yeah. But I think you'll like what I got in mind."

Slocum heard her fierce whispers. It was clear she didn't want him in the house.

"But if the missus don't want me," he said calmly, "I'll just drop it."

As Slocum thought, the sheriff took this opportunity to assert his manhood. He had been browbeaten enough in private, but he would not stand for it in public.

"You jus' wait. I'll come right down. Five minutes ain't the end of the world," Hamilton said, speaking both for his wife's and Slocum's benefit.

Soon the door opened. The sheriff scratched a match and lit the kerosene lamp on the table.

"New shade?"

"What? Oh, yeah. After you left I fell against the goddamn thing and busted it. Wife *never* saw her father drunk, she told me."

Slocum sensed the annoyed bitterness in the sheriff's remarks. He shrugged.

"A man has to howl once in a while," he observed.

"*You* try tellin' her that, Sheridan. Well, what's so important?"

Slocum jerked his chin upward.

"Oh. She can't hear. Even when the bedroom's door's open, you can't hear what people say down here. Except when you bust a lampshade an' fall off a chair. Then you never hear the end of *that*. Sit down."

So they weren't getting on well. Slocum found that interesting. He filed the fact away for future reference.

"Sheriff, I been thinkin'. Those two detectives. We had a little run-in t'night. Nothin' serious. No one hurt. It's all straightened out. No hard feelin's. But when it was over—they went their way, I went mine—I started thinkin'."

"Go ahead," said Hamilton, intrigued. The light made the bottom part of his face yellow; the green glass shade placed his face from the nose upwards in a green gloom. He looked gangrenous.

That, thought Slocum with a vicious pleasure, is the way he's going to look when he'll be dead a week. With my help.

"Sooner or later," Slocum said, "the three of us are gonna lock horns. Where do I stand if they get shot?"

"You mean killed?"

"Yeah."

"Think you c'n do it?"

Slocum shrugged. He was surprised to see that the sheriff seemed pleased at the idea that Slocum could kill the two Pinkerton men.

"You got nothin' to worry 'bout," Hamilton said with a faint smile. "Plenty of people seen 'em pushin' you 'round before. You got a perfect right to defend yoreself. Jus' make sure you do it in public." He grinned. Then he suddenly seemed indifferent; Slocum thought he looked as if he had something more important on his mind. He got up, took a bottle from the sideboard and poured out two glasses. He shoved one across to Slocum, sat down and drank half of his at a gulp. He set down the glass and took a deep breath.

"Sheridan. I got an idea. Hear me out. It'll take care of the Pinks. You won't have to worry 'bout them tryin' to force gunplay on you no more."

"Go ahead," Slocum said, very interested.

"The Pinks think they know the Territory. But I know it better than they do."

"That's the god-honest truth," Slocum said with sincerity. Cutting him off after he had robbed the train months before certainly did prove to Slocum that Hamilton had an expert knowledge of the Territory.

"Now," said Hamilton slowly, "my idea is gonna make us very rich. Very rich. Or we'll wind up doin' time."

"What?" Slocum said, startled.

"Jus' lissen, Sheridan. You jus' hear me out, now. The Dirty Dog stage comes down into Socorro every so often."

So Hamilton was planning to rob the stage! Slocum suppressed his glee. Let the man think that he had come just to complain about the Pinkertons. There would be no need for Slocum to make any suggestions. For a second Slocum thought it was wonderfully coincidental, but on quick reflection he changed his mind: After all, if a delicious apple pie is being baked and set on a windowsill to cool, why, there's bound to be lots of greedy small boys in the backyard thinking how to swipe it.

He would not have to spend time and energy urging a reluctant Hamilton to move. And it was far better this way. Hamilton, since he had produced the idea himself, would have a stubborn fondness for the project; he'd be eager to overcome any problems which might come up. Slocum silently blessed Mrs. Hamilton for her help. For, by her constant nagging pressure for more money and her desire to live in a fine, big city, she had unwittingly pushed Hamilton to take this decisive move.

"Ever since it got robbed couple months ago," the sheriff went on, "they plan to put four men on 'er. All good shots. I *know*. I recommended 'em. They'll be carryin' Winchesters. *An'* shotguns. An' they're *good*."

Hamilton was knocking his box of matches back and forth across the oak tabletop by alternately snapping each thumbnail at it. He kept his gaze focused on the box as he spoke, as if he were too embarrassed to look at Slocum directly.

"An' since they're good, we'll need *four* good men ourselves. Know who I got in mind?"

Slocum shook his head. It was all Hamilton's show.

"The Pinkertons. That stage carries a powerful lot o' bullion, Sheridan. I been thinkin'. Now, I'm pretty sure they'll never expect an attack on it in 'xactly the same place, an' done 'xactly the same way. People are dumb. They go 'round sayin' lightnin' never strikes twice in the same place. Bullshit! I seen plenty big trees out in some meadow been hit twice, even three times by lightnin'. So my idea is to hit 'em right smack in the same place."

Slocum liked the idea. He had pondered it, too.

"An' since they lost two million last time, they're gonna send out a big shipment this time, the manager tole me."

"Two million?" Slocum said, looking surprised. "I heard it was close to half a million."

"Bullshit. It was two million. Believe me."

"Mebbe you're right."

"Damn right I'm right. This time they're gonna

ship down jus' as much. 'Nother reason they're puttin' on four top men. To make sure no one's gonna try for it." He smiled. "But *I'm* gonna know jus' when it's comin'."

Slocum nodded. "I got jus' one question so far. Why d'you want *me?*"

Hamilton resumed his little game of volleying the matchbox back and forth with his thumbnails.

"Because you're the man who robbed the first Dirty Dog stage, Sheridan."

Slocum knew he had to play it very cool from now on. Was all this an elaborate plot to attempt to lure him into admitting the robbery? It would give the sheriff the prestige of a top-drawer arrest. But for several reasons Slocum didn't think this was so. First of all, there had to be at least one other witness to the admission. Was it possible that someone was hiding in the kitchen or out in the hallway? No, impossible. The kitchen window was open. Perhaps someone was crouched underneath it? Slocum stood up abruptly, took three fast steps, snatched the door open. No one there. He turned to face the honestly surprised sheriff.

"Left my cigars in the saddlebag. Be right back."

He closed the door and headed for the stable. The little excursion would give him a little more time to think. The second reason why it wasn't likely that all this was a plant was the amount of the reward. It was just too small. Especially since it probably would have to be split with the Pinkertons, who certainly would be supplying Hamilton with evidence and some legwork.

He walked into the stable. His horse, recognizing him, stamped and swung his muzzle around to face Slocum. Slocum patted him absentmindedly and pretended to fumble inside the saddlebag. There had never been any cigars there, but Hamilton might very well have followed him out of skepticism. Like Cameron, the sheriff was very light on his feet.

Slocum let the flap fall shut. He took his cigar case

from his inside pocket, took out a cigar, restored the case, and walked back with the unlit cigar in his hand.

The third reason was he didn't think it was all a trick was that corroboration was impossible without Cameron. And independent proof would be, of course, if they were to find the money either by following him, which was also impossible—*no one* could follow Slocum across desert country without his becoming aware of it immediately—or finally, by torturing him until he gasped out the hiding place.

That was a possibility. It would have to be kept in mind.

Fourth reason: If the election for sheriff would be next week, why, *maybe* Hamilton might be considering a good arrest—with all the favorable publicity—very definitely worthwhile.

But the election was two years away. And Hamilton, as Slocum had learned, was too cynical a politician to think that the citizens of Socorro County would remember the capture of Slocum that long. Besides, too many people detested rich mine owners. Some people might actually resent his capture.

No. Hamilton was after the hot apple pie—*if* he could get away without being suspected. Slocum decided to help him along.

He entered the kitchen with the cigar in his hand and sat down. Hamilton scratched a match aflame and lit the cigar for him. Slocum nodded his thanks, leaned back and crossed his arms.

"What makes you think I did it?" Slocum asked.

Hamilton grinned. "Because you're smart. Because you didn't go to Chicago. Because Cameron ain't around."

"What's Cameron got to do with it?"

"I *know* Cameron. He wasn't smart enough to think it up. But he knew when the shipment was due, workin' in my office. An' he wasn't around either at the time of the robbery."

Slocum grunted and took a long pull at the cigar. "An' I bet I know what happened. You jus' lissen, you don't have to say nothin'. You pulled it off with Cameron. He double-crossed you right away an' took off with the bullion. So you came back here, dead broke, an' kept on gamblin', buildin' up a stake, until somethin' interestin' comes along. Or until you run into Cameron again."

Hamilton smiled, pleased at his analysis. Slocum thought it wasn't at all a bad example of good thinking. Question was, how much of this outline had the Pinkertons supplied? And how much did they believe? Or had they fed careful little doses to Hamilton, wanting him to believe that Slocum was broke? That way, they might still get him somewhere and force him to reveal where the bullion was. If they thought he knew. Caution was the password for Slocum, and he damn well realized it.

Hamilton took Slocum's silence for assent.

"I know what I'm talkin' about. Cameron was very big on double-crossin'. I know stories 'bout that, but all I'll tell you right now is that I found out he was holdin' out on me when he was collectin' from the saloons." Hamilton shook his head in disgust. "So if he comes back here, I want first crack at 'im. But I don't think it'll happen. If he's got any sense left, which I doubt, he's smokin' big Havanas with a gal on each knee. Yep. An' he's investin' in good minin' stock, an' streetcar stock—that's the comin' thing—an' municipal bonds."

Hamilton's eyes were glowing with excitement. No, Slocum thought, this man is either the greatest actor in the world, or he *really* wants a crack at the next Dirty Dog stage with all that beautiful ductile and malleable metal.

"An' downtown property in a town like Frisco or Seattle!"

Hamilton squeezed the matchbox unwittingly. It

suddenly burst into flame. He slapped out the flame, but a charred spot was left on the tabletop.

"Mrs. Hamilton won't like that," Slocum observed.

Hamilton looked at it indifferently. "It's not going to matter in a little while," he said. "Look at Cameron. He don't ever have to bust hosses no more or kick fool cows outta mudholes. All he's gotta do—if he got good advice—is to clip coupons an' attend directors' meetin's. An' I bet he's got hisself a nice house somewheres an' servants an' a couple swell spans o' trotters in his stable." He sighed.

None of these fantasies was Slocum's idea of what a man should do with his life, but he could see the images drawn appealed enormously to Hamilton. The man tried to keep the excitement out of his face, but Slocum knew that Hamilton wanted that bullion so bad he could taste it. What he wanted now was the absolute assurance it could be pulled off safely and that he would be able to get away with his share.

"But," Slocum said judiciously, "we gotta look at it all around."

He knew that the way to reinforce Hamilton's plan was to draw a picture not only of vast and easy riches but a perfectly logical and secure manner of acquiring them.

"Sure, sure," Hamilton said.

Slocum saw that the man's eyes were fixed on the middle distance. I know what the dumb sonofabitch is thinking, Slocum thought. He's seeing himself step out of his Nob Hill mansion. He's wearing a derby and a fat gold watch chain and a watch that chimes the quarters and the halves as well as the hours. Mrs. Hamilton is clinging lovingly to his arm. She's wearing the latest Paris gown. She is looking up at him adoringly. Their pair of matched grays trot up. Their footmen salute. Yep, Slocum thought, the sonofabitch has a transparent face. Slocum waited patiently. He had waited months for this moment. A few more minutes wouldn't matter.

"Yeah, go ahead," Hamilton said hurriedly, forcing himself back to reality with a visible jerk.

"First of all," Slocum said, "nobody is gonna trust nobody. You or me or the Pinks. That isn't nice to say, but it's true."

"That's right," Hamilton said grudgingly, but full of respect for Slocum's blunt honesty.

"So, we got to build in what I call insurance policies."

"Go on," said Hamilton. He was fascinated.

"We all have to know each other. We have to know each other's plans. If we all got something on each other, then the other man's got something on us. Stands to reason. Anyone hold out or talk, well, we know enough to get even, you see? That way we all got confidence in each other. Because whenever a lot of money is floating around, people are going to be very suspicious. Very, *very* suspicious. Double-cross is gonna be in the air."

"Right."

"Next, we have to make sure that nobody connects you with it. With passin' on the information 'bout the time the stage is due here."

"How do we handle that?" Hamilton looked worried.

"Easy. All 'round where we're gonna jump the stage, we leave signs provin' we been there for days jus' waitin' for her to pop up. Ol' campfires, empty tin cans with food scraps still stuck in 'em, fresh horse turds. Spilled oats."

"Oats?"

"Sure. If the robbers took oats along, it means they knew there wasn't enough grass to keep four horses alive for a week or more. So they took oats. An' if they waited a week—an' if ever' one of us was in plain view here in Socorro for all that time—how could it be us who robbed the stage?"

"But how——"

"I'll go on up there early. Scatter tin cans 'round, build some fires, scatter oats an' horse turds. Day before robbery, you go on up to Albuquerque on business. The two Pinks go somewhere to look for ranch property."

"What about you?"

"A couple days before I'll get a telegram from my sister Martha askin' me to come to Chicago to help with a lawsuit 'gainst the estate. I'll write her tellin' I'll be along real soon. Then I'll hop the train, hop off in Albuquerque to wait for the Chicago train, buy a ticket for Chicago, but I won't get on the train. I'll change clothes an' hop the train for Gallup instead. I'll buy horses, burros, oats, supplies, blankets an' old clothes an' boots."

"Ol' clothes?"

"Sure, ol' clothes. We'll all wear somethin' different. Right afterwards we c'n change to our regular clothes."

"Say, that's smart!"

"Yep." Slocum suppressed a grin. It was the deal with Cameron all over again.

"I'll swing on back to the south side of Cebollita Mesa. No one ever goes there. There's plenty of water and grass from the mesa all the way to the stage road. You come out of Albuquerque an' meet me. We'll meet the Pinks an' get ready. Next mornin' it'll be over fast. We'll split up the bullion an' ever'one goes his way. Takes his own burros, each with his load. Bury it wherever you want. No one sees you 'cause we've all split off in different directions. You go back to Albuquerque an' take the train back to Socorro. I go on to Chicago. The two Pinks go on lookin' for that goddamn ranch. They don't even have to come back to Socorro. You come back to where you buried your share, maybe in a month, maybe two, three, whenever you think it's safe. You take it whenever you want. Maybe you jus' leave it lay until the next election. You campaign lousy an' you lose. You say you're gonna try your luck elsewhere. You sell your house, pull up stakes and go. Natural, right? Who'd ever think you had anythin' to do with the robbery? In the meantime you personally track down all the leads people give you—an' you jus' sadly tell the Dirty Dog people none of 'em panned out. See how nice? If you get a good lead, you jus' sorta don' try too hard. You lose the election an' take the missus somewheres nice an' live easy. How's anyone gonna tie any of us in? *I* don't see how."

He leaned back and lit a cigar. Hamilton was no longer leaning back with his arms folded. His elbows were on the table edge and he had pressed forward, greedily drinking every word.

Slocum paused.

"Go on," Hamilton said impatiently.

Slocum struck another match. His cigar had gone out. He puffed away, watching Hamilton. The man was jittery because of the delay. Slocum thought he looked like a child who had a favorite fairy tale which he loved; now that it was over, Slocum had the feeling that if he were to repeat it word for word, Hamilton would drink it in just as greedily as the first time.

Slocum shook out the match. "That's it," he said. "See if you c'n pick holes in it. I'm goin' back to bed. Adios."

He stood up and stretched.

"Maybe it'll be best if people don't see you an' me talkin' from now on," Hamilton said.

"Good idea," Slocum said, deliberately putting a note of admiration in his voice.

"Sunday's day after tomorrow. We c'n say hello

casual-like after services. I c'n give you my answer then."

"Fine. Take your time. See you Sunday."

"Sure, sure."

When Slocum opened the back door to leave, he turned around for a last look.

Hamilton was sitting motionless. His palms were flat on the table. He was staring unseeing at them. There was a smile at the corners of his lips. Slocum knew that the man was already spending his share of the bullion.

30

Slocum picked up his laundry next afternoon at Yee's.

"Sheridan!" Byron's voice called in back of him. Slocum's back muscles hardened involuntarily, as if the rigid muscles could protect him from a bullet in the back. Then he turned slowly.

Byron stood in the doorway. His hands were empty.

Slocum let his breath out slowly.

"Sheridan. I—well, I want to 'pologize f'r last night. Had too much firewater."

He seemed sincere.

"Sure," Slocum said, masking the wariness in his eyes.

"I musta been crazy. I sure am glad I missed. I mean, shootin' at someone when I was drunk! So I'm glad you unnerstan'."

"Yeah," Slocum said politely, "I been wild on panther juice myself once or twice."

Byron still stood in the doorway, not moving. Slocum felt uncomfortable. He didn't care for apologies. If they were to be made, he liked them short and to the point. This long drawn-out performance was not to his taste. He had known drunks who were sorry in the morning, and there was something about Byron which did not ring true.

"Any luck in ranch property?"

Byron shrugged. "You ride here an' ride there. A man says he's got six thousand head an' three creeks runnin' brimful year 'round. All right. You ride over practic'ly every goddamn acre. You ride in an' out of draws an' arroyos. You climb up mesas. An' you be goddamned if you c'n figger out how the ranch has got more 'n five thousand. An' it ain't three creeks always runnin'. It's one. An' that one runs right through some alkali flats. You're gonna have to sink some deep wells. You been ten days there an' it's all wasted time. There's an awful lot of liars 'round this here part of New Mexico."

Oh, how true that is, Slocum thought.

"So you hear 'bout 'nother ranch. Full of gramma grass, nice line of cliffs the cattle c'n run up under comes a blue norther. We ride over for a look. We don't find gramma but we sure do find sagebrush. The cliffs turn out to be ten feet tall an' the snow'll jus' whip off 'em an' right onto their backs. 'Nother ten days shot to hell!

"So that's the way things are. That's why we get drunk an' mess up," Byron concluded. "Any luck gamblin'?"

"Not so good these days."

"That's a good-lookin' pair o' boots."

"I'd spend my last cent on good boots faster'n pants or a hat."

"Don't blame you, Sheridan. Feel the same way myself. An' that's a mighty good-lookin' pony, that chestnut of yours. That's no ten-dollar piece of wolf-bait."

So, Slocum thought, he's trying to see if he can set up a connection between the money I win at poker and what I spend. If I spend more than I win, he's some sort of proof maybe I did the stagecoach job.

"Next to boots," Slocum said casually, "a man's gotta have a good horse between his legs. Never know when some cowboy's gonna see that extra ace fallin' out of my sleeve. I'm gonna have to change my address in fifteen seconds."

"True, true," Byron said, genuinely amused. "A real fast pony. I'm sorry to hear your luck's been pretty bad. Musta been better once?"

He's heavy-handed, Slocum thought. He's given up on being very careful. He must be getting sick of this job. That's probably why he's been drinking. He's plain bored.

"Sure," Slocum said. "I've had runs of good luck. One night, up in Gold Hill, up near Virginia City, I broke the faro bank for twenty-seven thousand dollars."

"Hey, that's good!"

The news lit a tiny spark of interest in his eyes. Slocum sensed it immediately. In a flash he decided to seize the opening. He knew how he could harrow and fertilize the ground for Hamilton.

"Had even better luck, up near Butte. A real nice place. Roulette this time. I walked away with a hundred and four thousand."

"Jesus Christ!"

"Yep. As I live an' breathe."

"I bet you lost it all next night."

"Nope. Went to San Francisco. Took me the best gal outta the best fancy house. I dolled 'er up real nice. We had champagne an' roast guinea hen till it came out of our ears. Blew it all in three months. But if I had to do it over again, I'd jus' take it all straight to Mexico City, an' put it all in railroad bonds an' live real nice."

"Railroad bonds?"

"They're buildin' railroads all over Mexico, an' they're bringin' a better return than savings banks or even handlin' cattle. Railroad bonds for me! I'd live real nice down there. You c'n get yourself a pretty li'l maid down there for a dollar a week. They cook your food an' scrub your back an' climb into bed with you, all for that dollar."

"For a dollar?"

"Yep. The U.S. dollar goes an awful long way down there—way better than along the border. An' the Mex guvvamint treats us American investors real nice."

"Well, well," Byron said ironically, "look who's comin'."

Slocum looked up. Hamilton was coming down the street at a fast trot. He was well dressed as usual, freshly shaven, nodding and smiling. The horse was a black gelding, 16 hands high, with a powerful chest. It would have to be a big horse to carry all that weight. But it was well groomed and had a glossy black skin with a high polish. The sheriff wore glistening black boots, almost a match for his horse. Little clouds of dust spurted up from each hoof. The horse had been well fed, was frisky and carried his head well up. A dog barked at him, and he went into a funny little dance, well controlled by the sheriff, who seemed to be in a fine mood. He nodded politely as he passed the three men. Teamsters cracked their whips as their heavy wagons creaked by, loaded with timber for the Dirty Dog mine tunnels and adits. Two more wagons followed with cast-iron sections for new stamping mills up at the Dirty Dog. They moved slowly and painfully. They would have a bad time going up the mountain roads.

"You c'n see that damn Colt bangin' up an' down," Byron said. "Some day he'll go somewhere with that and somebody will use the butt of it to lay his head open, jus' to see if there's anythin' inside."

"Well, Byron," Slocum said, "I got to be goin'."

They shook hands.

"No hard feelin's?"

"Nope."

He remembered the smell of gunpowder coming off his coat the night before when he removed it. Just the thought of it made him tense. He had plenty of hard feelings and he fully intended to collect for them. But what he had to do now was get out of the way so that Hamilton could have his private little conversation.

31

"It has pleased the Divine Dispenser," said the preacher, "to order us to accept his Divine Justice, no matter how seemingly revolting and terrible. It is not for us to question His commands. It is not——"

Oh, bullshit, thought Slocum wearily. He sat in the middle of the congregation next to the aisle. He wore his new boots and his newly pressed coat. Though the tailor had sponged the coat, it still reeked of gunpowder. If I had done what the preacher had advised, he thought, I'd be stretched out of Boot Hill in the cheapest coffin the town of Socorro could buy. Worst-grade pine, full of knotholes. Not that Slocum cared much. He didn't give a damn about being lowered in a mahogany casket with bronze handles, but he would like something better than knotty pine. Clear pine, for instance. He grinned at the thought.

The community had not yet been able to build a proper church. This had been a small warehouse, and it had been willed to the Methodist Congregation. They had chipped in and painted it white inside and out, bought some battered old oaken pews from a rundown neighborhood in Philadelphia, nailed on a five-foot steeple in the center of the flat roof and were busily engaged in soliciting funds for a bell.

Farther up the aisle, on the right side, sat Hamilton and his wife. She sat on the aisle. Her profile was lifted towards the pulpit. Her white-gloved hands were clasped together. Her ankles and knees were firmly pressed together. A brown wide-brimmed straw hat covered most of her hair. Mrs. Hamilton was an Episcopalian and had sense enough to keep quiet as to her real feelings about the congregation and the church, since she knew that their appearance there on Sundays was a political and not a religious act.

A child cried back of Slocum. Mrs. Hamilton turned around to look. She caught Slocum's direct, naked stare. She flushed and immediately faced the pulpit again. One thing was damn sure, Slocum thought. He was damn well going to push that redheaded woman on her back before he left Socorro for good.

The sermon droned on and on. Slocum fell asleep. He slept without any noise whatsoever. Always when he woke it was to full, immediate awareness. Now he woke up to the energetic jabbing of an old lady's elbow into his left side.

"Sorry, ma'am," he said, and stood up. The sermon was over. The sheriff was going past with Mrs. Hamilton on his arm. She deliberately kept her eyes on her husband's face so she wouldn't have to acknowledge Slocum's presence. He grinned and followed them outside.

The townspeople and the ranchers' wives were chatting in their usual excited Sunday fashion, scattered about the hard-packed earth in small groups. Hamilton waited until his wife was engaged in conversation. Then he moved away from her, nodding and speaking a few words here and there until he was next to Slocum.

"Mornin', Mr. Sheridan."

"Mornin', Sheriff. Nice day."

"Might rain this afternoon. The corn sure could

cuse a good fence-lifter. I had a talk yestiddy with a couple ranch people. Very interestin'. You might wanna come by t'night for some coffee an' some home-made apple pie." He raised his voice a trifle as he noticed the pharmacist coming close.

"Sure, Sheriff. I might be interested. S'pose I drop by tonight an' see what you got in your stable."

"Fine, Mr. Sheridan. Jus' fine."

Hamilton nodded and turned back towards his wife. She had been scanning the crowd and had caught sight of Hamilton talking to Slocum. She was staring at them with a hard, angry expression. As her husband stood next to her, it was clear to Slocum, from her frequent annoyed glances in his direction, that she was talking about him. And not in a complimentary manner, either.

"I thought they'd grab it right smart," said the sheriff. "But they din't."

"Why not?"

They were sitting around Hamilton's round table.

"First, they thought I was makin' up ev'rythin'. They thought the Dirty Dog people hired me to go 'round an' try an' persuade *them* to rob the stage. Now why the hell would anyone want to do *that*?" He shook his head in wonder.

Slocum knew very well what Byron meant by saying he'd like to open up Hamilton's head with his own gun to see if there was anything inside. A suspicious man with a detective's training in undercover work would automatically assume that his loyalty was being tested.

"What you say?"

"What did I say? I said, 'What the hell would I do *that* for?' " The indignant, astounded tone in Hamilton's voice was perfect. It would have convinced a far more astute man than Byron that such a thought had never crossed the sheriff's mind.

"Next," Hamilton went on, "they wanted to know who you was. I mean, I tole 'em I had someone who was real smart, a man who thought of ever'thin'. I wouldn't tell 'em who. I said, 'You wanna come in, fine, you say so an' you'll find out ever'thin'. So then they wanted to know if whoever it was wasn't workin' for the Dirty Dog."

"Oh, christalmighty!" Slocum said. He hadn't figured on such a wary, suspicious reaction. But he *should* have thought of it, he told himself. He had built himself a successful criminal career throughout the west just by thinking out such matters carefully. It was his fault for not foreseeing such details, and he determined not to be caught this way again.

"I tole 'em," said Hamilton, "that it was all gettin' too goddamn complicated and mebbe we ought to drop the goddamn thing. But when they thought over what they could grab for themselves an' when they thought what they was pullin' down workin' for Pinkerton—why, the Pinks was a gone goose."

Good thinking on their part, Slocum thought.

"Then what?"

"Then Hogan said to get rid of you. Then we'd take one-third each."

Oh ho, Slocum thought. They could hold their own in a pond full of eels.

"I tole 'em we ain't ditchin' the man who planned it all. Then they wanted to know why only fifteen percent each, while I get fifty an' you twenty. We ran that 'round the maypole till I got real tired an' real mad. So I said we'd talk some more tomorrow."

"Greedy sonsabitches. But we need 'em. When you see 'em again offer 'em twenty percent each."

"What?"

"Sure. Fifteen percent was only to see what they'd say. They said the hell with it, they wanted thirty-three and a third percent each. All right. We'll come up a little. Shows we're reasonable people to work with."

"What happen to my fifty?"

"You keep it. Just take away ten percent from me. I'd be satisfied with that. We *need* 'em."

The sheriff stared at Slocum.

"There's gonna be an awful lot of money," Slocum said. "You deserve your fifty. Without your information none of us would have a goddamn cent. None of us is married. You need the money more'n we do. Only fair."

"How 'bout the burros an' supplies?" Hamilton asked.

"You an' me'll put up two hundred each."

"What about them?"

"They're so crooked they ain't gonna believe you if you ask 'em for their share. They'll think you made up the whole thing jus' to swindle some money out of 'em. All you'd do is scare 'em off. We can collect afterwards for their share."

"That's it, then?"

"That's it. All you gotta do is tell 'em they're gettin' a bigger cut. They'll be happy their bluff worked, so they'll go along. Tell 'em they'll be asked to pay their share of the expenses after we split the bullion."

"I don't like them sonsabitches, Sheridan. I don't get a comfortable feelin' when I talk to 'em. I jus' don't trust 'em."

"You bet. I don't either. An' I tell you somethin' else. They're gonna try to dry-gulch us when they think we're not ready. That way they'll make a fifty-fifty split. Because fifty percent each is better'n twenty percent each. Stands to reason."

"It damn well does, Sheridan!"

"That's why they'll play their little game first about

fifteen percent each not bein' so much. That's why they'll act as happy as a pig in shit when you tell 'em it's goin' to be twenty for each of 'em. They'll think you trust 'em, y'see?"

"Yeah." Hamilton's face looked agonized.

"I think it's gonna work," Hamilton finally said.

"It damn well *will* work," Slocum said with an air of calm assurance that Hamilton seemed to find very comforting.

"All right. I'll make 'em a better offer t'morrow."

"Make 'em think it's like pullin' teeth."

"You bet."

Slocum leaned back in his chair and looked at the sheriff. Hamilton was chewing his bottom lip, thinking hard.

"I better be goin'," Slocum said, pushing back his chair. The sheriff stood up and shook his hand warmly. The contact amused Slocum. Here Hamilton shakes the hand that will pull the trigger of the gun which will kill him soon. And the hand which would soon be cupping his wife's breasts and pulling her thighs apart.

Oh, Slocum thought as he went out the gate, life was often very funny.

32

Slocum decided to exercise the chestnut. His legs were healing nicely, but he was putting on too much fat. He walked the gelding through the town, past Hamilton's house, where a quick look showed that the buggy was not in the barn. Once past the corn and squash fields, he broke into a canter south along the river road to its junction with the road running alongside the little river that came down out of the mountains far to the west.

By the time he had reached a dense clump of willows the chestnut was sweating profusely. Slocum dismounted, slung the saddle over the trunk of a fallen tree, draped the blanket over a branch and walked the chestnut back and forth till he was breathing normally. By that time there were low purple clouds scudding before a strong west wind driving little dust whirlwinds in front.

The storm would clearly break before he could reach town. He moved deeper into the grove. The dense, interlocking branches would afford him and the horse some protection.

Lightning flared in the distance in the huckleberry-blue sky. The boom of thunder followed. The wind came, smelling damp. Slocum lit a cigar and leaned against a tree trunk.

Then he heard the swift clop of hooves accompanied by the hissing of rubber tires along the dusty road. It was a light buggy. It halted under the trees bordering the road.

Slocum looked casually. It was Mrs. Hamilton. He put out his cigar lest the smell of it be carried to her. She had pulled up her white cotton skirt, revealing her black stockings and midcalf-length, black leather buttoned shoes, and as he watched she jumped down as lithely as a young girl. She pulled off her straw hat, once under the shelter of the branches, and pushed back a few tendrils of her flaming red hair from her sweat-beaded forehead with the back of her left hand.

The rain burst suddenly, turning the white dust of the road to dark brown. The wind blew chill, and she folded her arms across her breasts and backed against a tree trunk. The intensity of the rain increased. Hailstones bounced from branch to branch. Wet splotches spread across her dress. She started to shiver as the rain hissed against the leaves.

"Darn it!" she muttered.

Slocum's laugh startled her. She spun around, terrified, but when she saw who it was her fear turned to sullen annoyance. She turned her back to him and stared at the road.

"This ain't the time to get uppity, ma'am," he said. "We're in for a long, hard storm. I got this here horse blanket. It ain't a Navajo, an' it smells pretty high of horse, but it'll keep us dry. You're welcome to half of it."

He lifted up one corner invitingly.

She shook her head.

"Suit yourself, ma'am." He sat on a dry log with the blanket around him like a tent. He was dry and comfortable. The rain continued to thrash down at the trees. Her dress grew more and more damp. A few hailstones forced their way through the leafy barrier and struck her. She winced painfully.

"It don't hurt under here," she heard Slocum say.

"All right," she said grudgingly. He opened one end like a huge black wing. She sat beside him on the log, carefully keeping as much distance as she could between them.

He brought his left arm around her shoulders with the blanket. He could feel her steellike rigidity.

"It's like midnight," she said stiffly. Slocum could feel her body through her thin cotton dress giving off heat like a stove.

"Goin' to be a long, hard rain," Slocum said. "Not like an eastern sprinkle."

Very gently he began to run his fingertips around the nape of her neck.

She pulled away and was immediately exposed to the rain, which was lashing the trees in a cold, wild fury. Slocum held up the blanket with a smile. She slid back, her lips set tight in anger. He pulled the blanket around her once more and began again to stroke the back of her neck with the most delicate possible circling of his fingertips. She remained still. Very slowly, as if she were a just-trapped wild mare, he moved the tip of his index finger until it was just under her right ear. The fingertip then followed the line of her jaw to her chin and then retraced its path.

Then he bent over and kissed her neck.

She shuddered.

He reached around and unbuttoned the top two buttons of her dress. Her hand came up to stop him, but by then he had pulled down her dress over her shoulder as far as the two opened buttons would permit. In the darkness of the storm her flesh shone like the inside of a freshly cut mushroom. He bent down and kissed her bare shoulder, darting his tongue around in little damp circles. Slocum knew she was afraid to let herself go.

He reached across and unbuttoned two more buttons. Her cotton chemise was cut low and straight across. He slid a hand inside her dress, and feeling the outward thrust of her left breast through the thin fabric of the chemise, he cupped it suddenly in his palm, calloused from years of handling horses.

Even through the cotton he could feel how swiftly the softness of the nipple leaped into rigidity, like a cherry still half-ripe. And exactly at the same time her breathing began to quicken. His face was pressed against hers.

"*Stop*," she said, with venomous intensity.

He could feel the heat coming off her cheek, almost as if she were burning with fever.

He slid his palm to her right breast. Its nipple also hardened instantaneously. With his thumb and first two fingers he gently twisted and rubbed the nipple. Up till then her clenched hands had been set stiffly on her thighs. She had kept her legs locked rigidly together.

He sensed, rather than was sure, that her body was turning towards him.

He reached upward under the blanket and pulled

her dress down to her waist. Then he gripped her chemise strap and pulled it down. When it reached the curve of her shoulder she wiggled her upper arm to help him ease it off. He pulled down the other strap. She helped him again, this time with an impatient shrug of her right shoulder. Now she was naked from the waist up. He rubbed and cupped her breasts for a minute. Then he bent down and took the nipple of her left breast into his mouth.

She quivered. He ran his tongue around the wide pink aureole surrounding the hard congested protuberance of the nipple, then he took as much of the breast in his mouth as he could. Then he slowly pulled his head away, seizing the nipple with his lips and teeth at the last possible moment.

She gasped convulsively and turned frantically towards him. Her hands came up and pressed his head against her breast.

"Oh, my God, my God, don't stop!" she muttered thickly.

Slocum kept it up for several minutes. When she began to squeeze her thighs together and thrust them apart again and again he knew she was ready.

He reached down and pulled up her skirt and chemise. She was naked underneath. He paused, somewhat startled.

She whispered, "Too hot." He ran his fingers lightly up past her knees, up past the black stocking tops, and up, slowly, up the silken white texture of the skin of her thighs. She was wet with excitement. He ran a forefinger along the edge of her labia and she gripped his back convulsively. Her pubic hair was drenched.

She brought her thighs together and imprisoned his hand between them. Slocum was surprised at the power of her thigh muscles. She grabbed his forearm above his imprisoned wrist and as she ground and rotated her pelvis she rammed her labia back and forth across his wrist. Suddenly, with a muffled scream, she had an orgasm.

She panted and opened her thighs. He withdrew his hand and cupping her breasts, he kissed them again. Soon she began her quick, excited breathing. He pulled her thighs apart. He suddenly bent down and kissed the firm flesh on the inside of her thighs. She began to push his head away, murmuring, "No, no."

He held her hand and darted his tongue inside her vagina.

"Oh. I never—don't do that. It's—please, don't. *Don't.*"

Slocum paid no attention. In and out his tongue went. She tasted tart. He dragged his tongue around the labia and around the clitoris, which he just touched with the tip of his tongue, like a butterfly lighting on a flower petal.

Her excitement redoubled. It ran through her entire body like electricity through a wire, Slocum thought, half-excited himself, and half reveling in the thought that part of his revenge was being accomplished at that moment.

"Oh, my God," she moaned. "Oh, oh, oh, oh."

He seized the clitoris between his teeth and gently chewed it. It seemed to him that it sprang up half an inch like a jack-in-the-box. He took it deeply into his mouth and swirled his tongue around it.

It was still raining and still dark under the purple mass of thundercloud. She suddenly stood up, flinging the blanket away. Slocum rose with her; he pulled off her chemise and dress in one swift overhead movement. He bent down and spread the blanket over the wet, sodden leaves.

She stood naked except for her high-buttoned black shoes and black stockings. Slocum stripped off his clothes, watching her as she unpinned her hair.

By the time he was naked, too, they were both wet

with the rain. They were so excited they weren't aware of it.

He took her in his arms as they slid to a kneeling position. He forced open her mouth and slid his tongue inside. She had never done that before, it was obvious to Slocum, and she gasped with startled pleasure. Their tongues slid around each other's; Slocum's part that observed all this suddenly thought of a time he had seen two snakes mating. His hardened penis lay flat against her stomach. She pushed her pelvis out in order to increase the pressure against her stomach. He took her hand and placed it on his penis.

She was shy, but he had made her so aroused with his lovemaking that she grabbed it and stroked it. He gripped her buttocks and kneaded them, making her rotate her hips and drive them forward against his penis. He took one hand away and stroked her clitoris until he had inflamed it again to a hard little erection. He slid another finger in and out of her vagina until the insides of her thighs were dripping once more.

The rain still fell on them, unheeded. It slid between them, oiling their bodies.

After a few minutes she fell over on her back. She parted her legs and cocked them high in the air.

He kneeled for a moment, looking down at her.

This was part of his revenge, and he wanted to remember it.

Her body shone wet and white in the darkness, like a peony in a June night. Her long hair lay piled in serpentine red coils around her head. Her breasts were thrusting upward, topped by their hard nipples. They looked almost black in the dim light leaking down from the clouds and from the sky in the west, where the storm had at last stopped.

The dark triangular patch of red hair lay open and wet, awaiting him.

She strained her arms upward. "Oh, please," she gasped. "Oh, please. *Please*. Now. *Now!*"

That's what he wanted. He had her all ready like a bitch dog in heat. She was begging for it. *That* was something he'd save to tell Hamilton some day.

He penetrated her. He had no idea that she would turn into an animal. She screamed when he rammed in all the way. She bit his lip. She locked her legs so tightly around his back that he couldn't move, and he had to break her grip by force. At the height of her orgasm, when she felt him ejaculating, she raked his back with her fingernails. She rocked her head violently back and forth. And suddenly she began sobbing.

Slocum rolled over and stared at her. She covered her face in her hands and kept on sobbing.

Now she's paying for her fun, he thought. She had her illegal and immoral fun and now she's going to feel guilty and she'll cry for a while. He despised people like that. The rain had stopped. The clouds had blown themselves out and the sun had broken through. There was a steady drip from the leaves.

"You better leave right now," he said coldly. "People see your buggy out there an' the sun shinin', they'll fret. You better get dressed fast. I'll wait here half an hour. Nobody'll connect us."

She began to dress, her face averted. Her clothes were drenched. She pinned up her hair and kept her face turned away from him. He smiled, but winced a bit at the pain from the lower lip which she had bitten in her frenzy.

Slocum dressed at the same time, staring at her body. She had a long, slender torso which he could appreciate better, now that he had an impersonal interest in it. Her breasts in profile had an upward tilt, with their nipples perched slightly upwards as well.

She turned her back on him as she buttoned up.

Now she *really* hates herself, Slocum thought. He looked at her slim back with an ironic smile. He himself made his choices and accepted full responsibility for whatever happened. He liked the proverb he had heard once down in Old Mexico, somewhere in Sonora: "Take what you want—but pay for it."

She made no gesture of good-bye. He watched her mount the buggy and ride off.

A good screw and good riddance to it. He squeezed as much water as he could out of the sodden saddle blanket. The movement made the fresh scratches on his back twinge. He looked back over his shoulder.

Damn it to hell, he thought. The bitch dug deep, and we were rolling in the dirt. He decided to stop in at Doc Eisler's and have the vet drench the scratches with plenty of iodine.

He waited half an hour, shivering in his wet clothes, disliking her more and more. By the time he reached Eisler's office, he was in a foul mood. He told Eisler he had found an abandoned house cat when he was swimming and the cat had panicked when he tried to pick it up.

"Oh," said Eisler. He hummed a Strauss waltz from his native Vienna with a skeptical tone as he took a cotton swab, poured a big dollop of iodine over it, and said, "Dis vill hurt like bloody hell, Mr. Sheridan."

It did.

33

"It's no good, Sheridan," Hamilton said. "They said they wanna see you before they go ahead." He nervously shoved the piles of chips around.

Only the two of them were sitting at the table. It was early in the afternoon. The bartender was polishing shot glasses and holding them up against the sunlight to see if they needed more work. From the rear of the saloon came the dry click of billiard balls.

Slocum didn't want to see the two men. He didn't trust them at all. His hope was that they would refrain from doing anything until they were absolutely sure that the bullion haul was all theirs. *That* would be the time to watch them. But it looked like he would have to talk to them. He couldn't see any other way out of it.

"Sure."

The sheriff sighed in relief.

"They said they'd be down at the loadin' pens, down a little ways out of town. You know where that's located?"

"Sure."

"They said they're gonna be there all afternoon."

"All right."

"You jus' tell 'em you had a talk with me. They'll know right away what you're talkin' about."

Slocum nodded.

"Hey, where'd you get that lip? Did somebody punch ya?"

Slocum nodded again.

"You keep it up," grinned the sheriff, "an' I'll have to run yuh in for disorderly. What does the other guy look like?"

"Hard to say. Spent most of the time horizontal."

"That's good," Hamilton chuckled. "Good way of puttin' it. What happened?"

Slocum shrugged as if the incident was not worth mentioning. "Oh, got up and skedaddled for home."

Hamilton stood up, waved to the bartender and walked out. After a few minutes Slocum got up, walked to Reilly's Livery Stable and had his horse saddled. He swung up easily and rode casually to the loading pens as if he were only out for an afternoon's exercise.

He trotted through town and across the railroad tracks. The pens ran from the tracks to the river. At that time they held close to three thousand bawling, thirsty cattle.

Slocum rode along the splintered fence. He eyed the cattle critically. He thought it would be simpler to rustle cattle than to fool around robbing bullion. It was much simpler. they were not guarded by marksmen with double-barreled shotguns and cattle were much easier to dispose of than bullion. Besides, no one murdered one another—well, not often—over a cattle-rustling deal; and if you got caught, it was only a couple years in the territorial prison.

On the other hand, he mused, you could buy a beautiful ranch down in Old Mexico and then stock it with the finest breeding bulls. You were set for life. You could fence the pastures and control your breeding till you could really turn out some superb stuff for the market . . . he laughed as he realized he was building himself fantasies just like Hamilton.

At one angle of the fence he saw the two Pinkertons. They were both sitting on the top rail, each chewing a stalk of alfalfa. Playing ranchers still.

They turned and watched him approach. They did not look surprised when he halted in front of them.

"Afternoon, Sheridan," Hogan said.

"Afternoon, gentlemen," Slocum said. "I jus' been talkin' to the sheriff."

Hogan turned to his partner with a triumphant grin. Then he turned back.

"I figgered," he said.

Far at the other end of the pens, some cowpunchers were prodding cattle up a loading chute into a cattle car. Morgan was sitting beside the car on a top rail, critically watching everything.

"Ol' man Morgan doin' some shippin'," Byron observed. "To your hometown."

"I miss Chicago a whole lot sometimes," Slocum said. He caught a tiny look of disappointment in Hogan's eyes. Slocum knew what that meant: He had hoped that Slocum wouldn't know what his reaction should be.

Byron grinned.

Old man Morgan suddenly stood up on the second rail, balancing his legs against the top rail. The cattle were moving too slowly. They could hear him shouting curses. Then the old man jumped up, clung to an overhead four-by-four timber and ran his big roweled spurs along the backs of two steers in the chute.

"*That's* the way to get 'em movin' fast," Hogan said.

"Pretty spry for an old man," Byron added.

"Sink a sharp spur in a cow's ass, that'll get 'em movin'," Hogan said.

"Or a good sniff at some oats," Byron went on.

"Speakin' of oats," Hogan said, "I hear you been spreadin' oats around yourself."

"Not oats. The promise of oats."

"Yeah. The promise of oats. An' I also hear you got it all figgered out. I mean, *really* figgered."

"That's right."

"I was jus' wonderin' a little," Hogan went on. "S'pose I went an' told the Dirty Dog people all about it. An' we go along with you people. An' when the time comes to jump the stage, me an' my partner wouldn't get shot at, 'cause the guards would recognize us. See? An' you an' the noble sheriff, the voter's pride, the upstandin' candidate from Socorro County—why, the both of you would get your heads blown off. Ever think of that?"

"Sure." Slocum's calm seemed to him to annoy Hogan.

"An'," Hogan went on, "we'd get a nice reward an' a nice promotion."

"I thought of that, sure."

"Well," Hogan demanded, with some sharpness, "why come to us? Ain't that a little stupid?"

"No."

"S'pose you tell us why not, Sheridan."

"Because you'd get maybe a thousand, two thousand bucks each. The Dirty Dog ain't throwin' money away. You'd get a handshake, a cheap gold watch, and a lollipop. You'd get your pictures in the papers. An' then you'd go out an' do another undercover job for the Pinks. An' sooner or later, you'd collect."

" 'Collect'? I don't get you, Sheridan."

"Collect. Collect a bullet in the heart. Or a leg blown off. Then you'd get a couple thousand bucks for that. You'd get yourself another handshake and a paragraph in the paper. If you're dead, you're forgotten. If you're still alive an' in a wheelchair, you're still forgotten. An' if you got one leg, maybe they'll buy you a wooden leg, an' you c'n spend your life swabbin' out saloons, like that broken-down ol' cowpuncher down at the Texas Star."

Hogan nodded reluctantly.

"On the other hand, s'pose you throw in with us. They won't expect us. *Not* in the same place, the same way. *We* don't move till we know for damn sure they're stickin' at least a million in that stage. An' the only man who'll know that for sure is Hamilton."

"You sound awful sure."

"I been around here an' there, Hogan. You try an' find a weak spot."

Byron nodded. "I tried," he said. "Ain't none. But our friend's not too smart."

"Smart enough to know 'bout the stagecoach. Smart enough to shoot if he has to. Smart enough to keep quiet. But as long as you're smart enough to get out of the country fast, what the hell's the difference?"

"Our friend says you'll have diggin' equipment."

"Everyone'll have his own pick an' shovel."

"Transportation?"

"I'll have good horses. Good burros. Plenty of oats to keep 'em movin' fast across bad stretches."

"Cost a lot of money. We don't have none."

"We figgered that. We need you. We're supplyin' ever'thin'. You jus' pay us back our expenses afterwards."

Hogan nodded.

Byron said, "I'm gettin' awful sick of ridin' 'round to all these goddamn ranches an' listenin' to them ranchers hand me their horseshit an' then goin' back to the hotel an' writin' those goddamn reports nobody reads."

"You got it all figgered out nice," Hogan said.

"Yep."

"Do you ever get the feelin' that you ever went through all that plannin' before?"

"Sure," Slocum said, drumming his fingers idly on his saddle horn. "I dreamed it all happened before."

"How did it all work out?"

"In the dream?"

"Yeah," Hogan growled. "In the dream."

"Oh, it went perfect. We buried the gold in a safe place. Found someone to buy it. A little at a time. In the dream, nacherly."

"So why did you come back? I mean, in the dream."

"In the dream I came back to Socorro to do it again."

"Alone?"

"My partner said he had enough. He scared easy. So he left."

"Where to?"

"I dreamed he knew people from the Confederacy who settled down ranchin' in Brazil. Or Argentina.

So he said he'd like to take up ranchin' down there."

"So why did you come back?"

"In the dream?" Slocum asked patiently.

"Yeah, yeah. In the dream, Sheridan."

"I'm greedy," he said pleasantly. "I was sure they'd never dream—in *my* dream—that there'd be another holdup right smack at the same spot. An' that's a *good* spot. At least six, seven hours got to pass before they c'n get a posse together. That gives us at least ten hours head start. On well-rested, well-fed horses. Carryin' plenty of oats for that stretch across the lava beds. Sure as shootin' they won't have no oats or water for their horses. We'll have all that. So I dreamed if I could get some good men together—enough to take care of the extra guards they been carryin' ever since the robbery—why, we'd all do mighty well."

The two men thoughtfully chewed their alfalfa stalks.

Byron said, staring at the river, "How 'bout it?"

"Why the hell not?" said Hogan.

34

Two days later Hamilton got word from the mine manager. The bullion would be shipped on September 14. That gave Slocum ten days to prepare.

From a horse dealer Slocum bought a cheap, sway-backed ten-year-old mare. He did not plan to ride it away from the holdup: Then he would have his choice of three better ones. The burros were another matter. He bought eight good, strong ones. He bought picks, shovels, canned goods, blankets, a frying pan and a kettle. He bought some flour and dried raisins. He bought canteens and water bags. He bought anything that would persuade anyone in town and anyone whom he would run across that he was a bona fide prospector lugging a lot of gear into the mining country for himself and his partners.

The same gear would also persuade his partners in crime that he was well prepared to carry out their plans for the Dirty Dog mine.

He rode his horse and let out his string of burros late in the afternoon. He had packed away his good boots. He wore new jeans. He packed a woolen shirt which would come in handy in the nights. The days were already beginning to get cool at the high altitudes he'd be operating in. Since his hands had softened up in the last few months he wore buckskin gloves. Lashing packs and dealing with recalcitrant burros in chill mornings could rip the skin off his palms.

He headed southwest. The trail left the wagon road and headed towards a distant mesa. He kept a sack and shovel handy. Every time he saw fresh horse droppings he carefully scraped them up and dropped them into the sack. He also saved all burro droppings and those went into another sack. It would not do to mix them together. Too many sharp eyes would be looking them over later and trying to figure out how come they were indiscriminately jumbled together.

Cliffs of Navajo sandstone rose hundreds of feet above the desert floor. Late in the afternoon some of their shadows were cast 30 miles by the slowly sinking sun. The cool of the shadows was pleasant. To emerge from the darkness into the full sun was like being struck by a club. Once, in such a desert, Slocum had been forced to live by soaking hardtack in his horse's blood. He made a face at the memory. He was riding hard to escape from a posse, and it had come to the point where he either killed his horse in order to survive with the liquid, and walked, or died of thirst. He killed the horse, but at a narrow place in the trail.

Afterward, he held the posse off by some well-placed shots and escaped in the dark by a 30-mile walk.

He watched the moon rise while the sun was sinking on the western horizon, a perfect enormous red globe. He could see 50 miles in every direction. Poised between the sun and the moon, the burros plodded patiently, their delicate hooves kicking up tiny clouds of dust which the wind promptly deposited on the blades of cactus beside the trail. Tiny green lizards, their legs pumping frantically, scuttled across the trail.

The sun sank behind a western ridge. The night hunters began to come out.

It was time to camp. He found water soon, and hobbling the mules, he fed them oats. He wanted them strong and ready to move fast with a load. No scurrying for whatever patches of grass they might find here and there.

He made a little fire, the kind an Indian would make, just the size of his two palms joined together. Nachodise had taught him how to do it. He fried some bacon. He had carefully packed along six eggs. He fried two of them in the bacon grease. He made some biscuit dough, wrapped it in a spiral around a green twig and shoved it into the coals to bake. He drank coffee.

The moon rose to its full height. He stretched out in his blankets in the chilly air. The moon was directly overhead and so bright that he had to cover his face with a corner of his blanket in order to sleep.

But although he was very tired, he couldn't doze off. He was thinking about Cameron. He thought of Idagalele. Her name meant "that which is becoming life." Nachodise did not know the English word, "pollen."

When he thought of her being shot in the stomach, he was sorry that Cameron had died so quickly, and without any personal boost from him to help him along to hell. But Hamilton would make up for it. He thought of Hamilton pulling on Bond's legs.

His old rage flared up the way it had not for weeks. He knew he wouldn't be able to sleep. He sat up, pulled on his boots, and stayed up all night, leaning against his saddle, rolling and smoking cigarettes and thinking out to the last detail exactly what he would do when the four of them would be assembled waiting for the stage to rattle up the hill.

The moon set. The stars began their powerful white pulsating flash, the way they only did in the high clear desert air. There was an occasional brief phosphorescent streak as a meteor slashed its diagonal across the sky.

Slocum noticed none of it. He was thinking. His thinking was hard and intense, and it surrounded the subject from all sides, predicting everything that could go wrong, determining, in each case, the best course of action. Usually a few hours of that complicated thinking ended up in a kind of absolute mental exhaustion, and Slocum would then fall asleep as if a switch had been turned off.

But not this time.

Hours passed. The sky paled and became washed out, the color of a very old blue shirt. Slocum had not slept at all. His arms were crossed, his legs were stretched out and all around his blanket were cigarette butts, each one viciously ground down.

He was angry. He stayed angry for the next five days. On the sixth day he reached the ambush area. There he proceeded to make several fires. He carefully spread the horse and burro droppings he had been collecting during the past few days.

He opened several tin cans, carefully and regretfully burying the food where it would not be found. He did not want the Pinkertons coming across it and complaining that it had been badly handled. When he finished, the scene looked as if several men had been waiting there for days.

He hobbled the burros and the horse. He had deliberately not fed them for two days. They were famished and ate up every green thing they could find in a hundred-yard radius of the camp. Good. It looked very authentic, Slocum thought.

Now all he had to do was wait for the three men to walk into the trap.

35

They showed up late next afternoon.

Both Byron and Hogan came riding across country. They were hungry and in a bad temper. It had rained that morning in the mountains and they hadn't thought to take slickers along. They said nothing when they saw Slocum. They dismounted with a curt nod. Slocum liked Byron's horse, a 16½-hands-high sorrel mare. He decided she would be the one he'd take.

While Slocum was making a quick meal for them of bacon and beans, Hamilton rode in. He refused food and hobbled his horse. He looked around at the grass situation.

"Your goddamn crow bait's et up all the grass worse'n some goddamn sheep," he sourly observed.

Slocum had carefully hidden the oats on which the burros and Byron's horse would be fed later. Besides, as he patiently pointed out, the grass *would* have to be eaten up so that the Dirty Dog people would be convinced that the robbers didn't know when the stage was coming. Slocum felt nothing but annoyance that it was necessary to repeat this to Hamilton. The Pinkertons understood this, and made no fuss about the scarcity of forage for their horses.

There was something about Hamilton's expression that interested Slocum. He kept staring at Slocum from under his half-lowered eyelids. His habitually reddish complexion was darker, partly by exposure to the sun and partly because it was suffused with some emotion. Slocum suddenly looked up and caught a look of pure hatred. Then she must have finally burst out and told the sheriff about him!

"How's the missus?" Slocum asked casually.

Hamilton opened both palms and rubbed them slowly on his thighs. His hands were sweating, even though the air at that height was cool. With great effort the man managed to keep his voice from trembling.

"Fine," he finally said. Slocum knew that the sheriff was certainly not going to bring up the subject of his being a cuckold in front of the two Pinkertons, who would be vastly amused by it. He would contain himself till later. And later, as Slocum knew, meant sometime after they had pulled off the robbery. Slocum thought with grim amusement that there was nothing like the prospect of a lot of money to keep a man from exhibiting public anger over a seduced wife.

The Pinkertons were standing by the fire. Their damp clothes were steaming. The heat of the fire made them feel better.

"We hit one of those big mountain storms," Hogan said. "The lightnin' went an' electrified the bob-wire. I got down to open a gate an' got knocked on my ass. Then I go an' ride standin' up to keep the seat of my pants dry an' what happens? My boots fill up with water.

"Then," Hogan continued, "we come upon a small band of Apaches. They was makin' cigarettes next to a crick. As soon as they seen us they took to their ponies an' lit out. I think they was a war party."

"What makes you think so?" demanded Hamilton.

Hogan looked at him, annoyed. "They wasn't fillin' up little tin pails with blueberries, that's for dang sure," he said curtly. Byron tittered, and Hamilton turned and gave him a sullen stare.

Slocum thought that he had never been with a group that so thoroughly disliked each other. It was time to put a stop to all this bickering.

"How many in the party?" he asked.

"Five. They followed us along a ridge."

"How far back was this?"

"Mebbe twenty miles. Think they're around?"

"If they were, they ain't anymore. Four men with guns, the odds are lousy."

"Sure?"

"Sure? I say they went off lookin' for someone easy. If I'm wrong an' they kill us, I'll be the first to 'pologize. How's that?"

"No call to git huffy, Sheridan."

"By God, as soon as you guys came here you begin' whinin' about this an' that. You want me to wet some rags an' make you all some sugar-tits?"

Nobody said anything.

Just stick around till tomorrow, thought Slocum. You're really going to have something to complain about then.

Slocum turned to Byron, who was busily stuffing beans and biscuits into his mouth.

"How come you ain't complainin'?" he asked.

"OK. Ain't 'nough salt in these here biscuits," he mumbled. Slocum sort of liked Byron, in spite of the fact that the man had tried to kill him recently.

Everyone laughed. Byron's remark cleared the air a little, but there was still a residue of tension left. Slocum didn't like the situation. It would put everyone on edge, and people were bound to be nervous enough being in such a dangerous venture as they were now engaged upon. It would make everyone doubly wary, more vigilant and more distrustful. He would have to reassure them. He sighed secretly. He thought it was worse than the night the pigs got loose in the girls' dormitory.

Byron got up and wandered about, munching on the last biscuit. He looked critically at Slocum's horse.

"Sheridan, that's some rotten hay-burner you bought yourself. I'm surprised."

"He moves fine, jus' fine. Don' worry 'bout him. Wait till we start movin' tomorrow. You'll see a real stepper." Slocum hunkered down and began scraping out the inside of the frying pan with a bunch of twigs.

"Looks like we really been here a week," Hogan said. "Pretty good, Sheridan. Where'd all the horse apples come from?"

"Mr. Sheridan's been talkin' to hisself while he was waitin'," Hamilton said viciously. "They come outta his mouth."

All three men turned to stare at him. This sudden impassioned outburst was not Hamilton's regular style.

Slocum slowly lifted his head. There had been people in Slocum's life who had seen the head come up just that way, with its cold, heavy-lidded green stare. Most of those people had died immediately afterward.

Byron and Hogan did not know of this, of course, but when they saw that look they instinctively stepped backwards. There were simply some people with whom you did not chance such remarks. Byron's mouth stopped chewing.

"Nope," Slocum said. "Ain't mine. The hoss is bored talkin' to me, so he spent all this time talkin' to himself."

Byron and Hogan burst into relieved laughter. Hamilton pulled off his saddle and dumped it angrily on the ground. He pulled off the saddle blanket, dragged it to a smooth spot and kicked the saddle roughly with the heel of his boot until he maneuvered it so that when he sat down on the blanket his back was to Slocum.

"I been sleepin' all day," he said idly. "I'll keep watch all night so you guys c'n catch up."

"No," Hamilton said, "we'll split the watch equ'l. It's only fair."

Hogan said easily, "I'm tired. So's Byron. So are you. He ain't, he's been restin' for days. We been movin' for days. Let him stay up all night. We're gonna need all the sleep we c'n get. T'morrow we'll be ridin' hard all day."

"Makes sense," Byron said.

Slocum watched Byron spread his bedroll, kick off his boots and pull his blankets up.

"When's the stage comin'?" he asked.

Hamilton said sullenly, tucking in the blankets, "It's leavin' at sunup. Oughtta be here 'bout ten."

"Good night, folks," Byron said cheerfully.

"Good night," Slocum said.

Hogan added his good night. Hamilton stared at Slocum, who calmly returned the stare until Hamilton dropped his eyes. After a while Hamilton began to snore. The three men were exhausted, and they slept well. Slocum watched them, smoking his cigarettes. He thought of a line from the Bible. *The Lord hath delivered mine enemies unto my hands.* A fierce jubilation seized him.

It was the slowest night he could remember. When dawn finally came, it was a delicate pale pink that reminded him of his mother's tea roses. The men still slept. Slocum let them sleep. At eight he made breakfast. They woke to the aroma of frying bacon and boiling coffee.

As they ate Slocum said, "Here's what we'll do."

36

Like the others, Slocum had not shaved for several days. His beard was beginning to itch. As he spoke he idly scratched his face. He noticed that the constant sullen look on Hamilton's face had been replaced by one of puzzled curiosity. Slocum did not like it.

"There's the rocks on the other side of the road," Slocum said. "See 'em?" One was ten feet from the road; the other several feet higher on the sloping ground and 40 feet farther down hill.

Byron and Hogan nodded.

"Byron, you get behind that one, the one close by. Hogan, you'll take the one farther down the road. Get yourselves nice an' comfortable." Slocum had picked the rocks carefully. He wanted them far apart as possible.

"Hamilton, you take that one. See it?"

"Where you gonna be, holdin' the hosses?" Hamilton demanded, with a sneer.

Byron looked disgusted. Slocum paid no attention. He went on.

"When the stage starts to climb the hill, I'll get out on the road. I'll sit down like I got a busted ankle. I'll pull off one boot an' I'll jus' be sittin' there, holdin' my leg an' lookin' plumb pitiful. They'll stop. They'll figger my hoss threw me an' took off. They ain't gonna throw down on me. One man, mebbe two, they'll bend down to help me."

"S'pose they won't? S'pose they figger it's a trick?" demanded Hamilton.

" 'Cause no one *ever* tried it before," Slocum said calmly. "I won't have no Winchester around. No shotgun. Whoever stuck up a stage with four guards totin' shotguns? An' a cowboy with a broken leg with only a Colt? They ain't gonna be suspicious at all."

"He's right," Byron said.

"When the guards bend down, they'll toss their shotguns back up on the seat or in the boot. When they bend over me I'll get the drop on 'em. As soon as I pull on 'em you three all yell 'Stick 'em up!' Now it'll be you three with shotguns right on 'em, an' there's only gonna be two men with shotguns now, the other two guards. Mebbe they won't even be carryin' 'em, they get too heavy, totin' 'em up that hill. They'll probably be in the boot, too. So the way it'll wind up, the four guards are only be carryin' Colts, see? An' when they see three shotguns leveled at 'em, they ain't gonna decide to be heroes. That's why I want everyone far apart. They'll think we're an army."

"Pretty good," Byron said. To Hamilton he remarked, "Any objections?"

Hamilton shrugged. Byron gave him a thin contemptuous smile.

The stage suddenly appeared on the crest of the opposite hill.

"There's our money," Slocum said. Byron and Hogan ran across the road to their respective rocks. Hamilton ambled over to the large boulder Slocum had picked out for him.

Slocum sat for a while. It would be 20 minutes before the stage would get close. He stood up and walked into the middle of the road, looking up critically at the rocks concealing the three men. He shook his head, as if displeased. He climbed up towards Hogan.

Hogan was stretched out flat. His shotgun lay beside him. "What's the matter?" he asked.

"I c'n see you from the road."

"Shit."

"Get back 'bout a foot."

"Sure."

Hogan started to wriggle back. Slocum stood in

back of him and took out the knife he had bought in Albuquerque ten days before. He had kept it in his saddlebag. He opened it. He had spent a long time honing both the blade and point to a razor sharpness. In his left hand he held a large stone.

"How's it now?" Hogan asked. He started to turn around.

"Fine," Slocum said, his voice cool. He hit Hogan on the back of the skull with the stone. He jammed the blade under the left ear and angled it upward into the brain. Hogan's unconscious body quivered convulsively and then was still. Slocum drove the wet blade into the soft dry soil up to the hilt. He pulled it out, folded it and slipped it back into his pocket.

He scrambled along the slope until he came to Byron's position.

"What's up?"

"I c'n see you easy from the road. Jus' back up 'bout two feet to your right."

Slocum stood back of Byron and took out his knife. He opened it. He bent down to pick up a rock, and was straightening up when Byron suddenly turned and looked up at him. Byron started to lift his shotgun, but Slocum kicked the barrel aside, dropped to his knees and swung the rock down hard at Byron's head. Byron jerked his head aside and the rock smashed into the boulder back of him. It made too much noise and Slocum was afraid that Hamilton might have heard it.

If he had, and investigated, things might start going badly for Slocum. He became angry for the first time, and felt a red haze beginning to settle over his vision, as it did when he began to lose control.

Byron tried to pull his barrel around for a shot, but Slocum fell across him, his left hand forcing the barrel aside and his right hand driving the knife in his throat up to the hilt. Byron strangled and shuddered, his face convulsed with hatred. His two hands came up to grab the hilt and pull it out, but they were too weak. He took a deep breath and opened his mouth. Slocum was afraid that he was going to yell. He clapped a hand across his mouth.

With the last bit of strength he had left, Byron bit it as hard as he could. Then he died.

Slocum, still on his knees, lest he be seen by Hamilton on the other side of the road, withdrew the knife and drove it into the ground. He left it there. It had done its work and he didn't want to look at it again. He felt a little sick. He didn't like knifing people. His hand hurt. Byron's teeth had broken the skin on both sides of the palm in a neat semicircle of bloody indentations. Slocum rolled over and lay on his back for a moment, taking deep breaths. His body was covered with sweat. When his heart stopped its wild racing, he got up and scrambled down the slope, walked up the road, and climbed up to the boulder behind which Hamilton was sitting with his back against another boulder.

Slocum was now in full control of himself.

"What was all that racket?" Hamilton's shotgun lay in the crook of his elbow.

Slocum grinned. "He got stung by a little scorpion," he said. "Sat down on one an' it bit 'im in the ass. He kept floppin' round an' cursin' till the daylight turned yaller, but he calmed down somewhat."

Hamilton smiled. He liked the idea of Byron being stung by a scorpion.

"Your gun loaded?" Slocum asked.

"What?"

"Your gun loaded?" Hamilton was peering anxiously down the road.

"Sure it's loaded! What the hell good would it be if it wasn't loaded? What kind of a fool question is that?"

"I've heard a lot of people say their guns was

loaded. An' when they pulled the trigger, it wasn't. They jus' forgot."

"Shitfire!" Hamilton said angrily. "Satisfy yourself."

He tossed the shotgun to Slocum and continued his tense inspection of the road. Slocum dug the muzzle into the ground and rammed two inches of the dirt into the muzzle. He wiped off the traces of the dirt around the barrel. Hamilton turned around and watched as Slocum broke it open, saw the shells, and pretending satisfaction, handed the gun back.

"Satisfied?" Hamilton asked contemptuously.

"Yep."

High above them a vulture was soaring. Slocum kept looking at it. It soared for six minutes without a wing-flap. Hamilton noticed it too.

"What the hell's that hangin' 'round for?" he muttered.

"Prob'ly spotted our garbage," Slocum said. "You ain't superstitious, are you?"

Hamilton refused to answer. The white and pitiless sunlight shimmered and shook unrestrained above the desert Slocum would be crossing later, all alone. A little green lizard ran vertically up the face of their boulder, stared at them, leaped off and scuttled away.

"We changed the plans a little," Slocum said easily.

"Jesus Christ Almighty! Ain't it late for that?"

"Nope. Byron said they'll get too suspicious, seein' me sittin' in the road. Said they'd get suspicious over anythin' right 'round here. Thought it over and reckoned he's right. He said the goddamn stage would run right over me. So we decided the best thing to do is for Byron an' Hogan to kill the lead hosses. At that distance they ain't gonna miss. When they go down, the stage stops. The guards'll be lookin' at their side. Then you an' me, we fire warnin' shots. When they hear them slugs whistle past, why, that'll tell 'em we're here on business. They won't see any of us. I'll tell 'em hands up. They ain't goin' nowhere with two dead hosses in the traces."

"Yeah. Sounds good."

Hamilton was pale. Slocum realized the man had never stuck up a stage before. They could hear the jingle and clatter of the stage coming up the hill. Slocum heard the clicks as Hamilton cocked both barrels of his shotgun. That wasn't good. The man was so nervous he might fire both shells and ruin everything.

"No good," Slocum said quietly. "Let the hammers down real easy."

"What?" Hamilton's face was even more pale.

"Here. Gimme your gun a second." He took it and gingerly let both hammers down. "Lissen, Hamilton," he whispered, "don't cock it until you hear them shoot. Time enough. Right?"

Hamilton nodded and swallowed.

"Remember. Wait till they shoot."

Hamilton stretched out flat and got a rigid grip on the shotgun. Slocum leaned back against the boulder back of him with his legs stretched out and his arms folded, his silver-decorated Colt in his right hand. He didn't bother to look at the road.

The jingling and the rattle of the stage grew louder.

The stage came around the bend. All the guards were walking. The load of bullion was very heavy. To make it easy on the horses, the guards got down at the foot of each steep hill and walked up. Slocum was pleased to see that his predictive abilities were still good: None was carrying a shotgun. He could see the four muzzles of the shotguns sticking up above the edge of the boot, close to the driver's legs. He could toss them out fast if he had to. The springs of the stage was squashed flat.

"My God," Hamilton breathed. "What a load she's carryin'!"

The stage came closer. Hamilton turned rigid. His hand moved towards the hammers. Slocum placed his hand on top of Hamilton's, and the man looked down, annoyed, and noticed for the first time the fresh bite marks on Slocum's palm.

His face showed puzzlement, but he directed his fascinated glance to the stage. His breath was coming in small stertorous puffs. His knuckles had turned white as he gripped his gun. The stage was 50 feet away. Then 40. Thirty. Slocum watched Hamilton's face. Twenty. Ten. The stage had already passed the boulders from which the two crippling shots were to have come.

Slocum didn't even look at it. He was concentrating on Hamilton's face, watching the range of expressions that succeeded each other. To Slocum it was better than any stage comedy he had ever seen. Wariness; nervousness; complete absorption; extreme rigidity of attention; bewilderment as the stage went by Byron and Hogan without their firing a shot; and finally, puzzlement.

As the stage came opposite them, Hamilton spun his head wildly to look at Slocum.

Slocum put his finger to his lips.

Once more Hamilton spun his head around to look at the stage. It was past them. Then he turned to look at Slocum. His face was filled with a mixture of rage and bewilderment.

"What——" he began, but Slocum once more placed a finger to his lips and pointed to the rear of the stage. Hamilton subsided, still bewildered.

When the stage had disappeared around the next bend, Hamilton leaped to his feet, shouting, "What the hell happened, you sonsabitches?" He ran down the slope, down the road, and scrambled up towards

Byron's dead body. Slocum let him go and watched him with sardonic amusement.

Hamilton scrambled up the slope, yelling furiously. He came to a sudden halt. He slid and fell, caught himself and started to run up the road towards Slocum, who simply pointed up towards the boulder behind which Hogan lay dead. Hamilton went up the slope once more, looked down and ran heavily, panting, down the slope. Slocum stood up leisurely and picked his way carefully down to the road.

"Holy Christ!" Hamilton shouted. "Holy Christ! They're dead!"

He was so rattled he didn't notice how calmly Slocum took the news.

"Yep," Slocum said impassively. Then he added, as curt as the crack of a stage-driver's whip, *"Hamilton!"*

Hamilton stopped as abruptly as if he had been reined in.

"I *know* they're dead," Slocum said. He dropped his hand onto his gun butt.

"It was Apaches!" He looked around wildly in every direction.

"No," said Slocum. "No. It wasn't Apaches."

"Then who was it?"

Goddamnit, Slocum thought, Byron was right. I'd like to really lay open Hamilton's head to see what was inside.

"*Not* Apaches," Slocum said.

"No?"

Somehow, Hamilton seemed calmer. It was as if thinking and talking about Apaches had the effect of soothing him. Slocum realized that to Hamilton the thoughts of a remote danger somehow took away the pressure of an immediate peril. It was a kind of thinking he had never indulged in, and he stared at Hamilton as if he were a weird animal in a zoo.

"No," he said finally. "It wasn't the Apaches. It was me."

Over Hamilton's face swept the most extreme look of puzzled bewilderment Slocum had ever seen in his life.

"Yeah, yeah," he stammered, "but why?"

"You don't know me, do you?"

Hamilton shook his head.

Slocum ripped his shirt till he had exposed his bullet-scarred shoulder.

"Look hard!"

Hamilton stood mute, uncomprehending.

For the first time since he had come riding back into Socorro from Silver City in a gambler's outfit Slocum dropped his Northern way of speech. He resumed his soft, slow Southern accent. It seemed to Slocum, even in his rage, that it was like getting out of an uncomfortable suit that fitted badly into an old pair of trousers and an old worn shirt.

"Look hard, you sonofabitch!"

Slocum ran his bleeding left hand over the stubble on his upper lip.

"Imagine me with a big black mustache! Twenty pounds heavier. An' no gray hairs. An' with a shoulder without a hole in it. Ever' time it got chilly that shoulder acted up, Sheriff. Take a good look at that scar, Hamilton!"

"Try hard. No? Now 'magine Ah'm 'bout to rob a train with a double-crossin' rat named George Cameron!"

Hamilton's jaw dropped. At the same time he swung the barrel of his shotgun around and pulled both triggers. Slocum had forgotten how fast Hamilton could move when he wanted. The muzzle was just two feet from the center of his chest.

The explosion of the gasses in the jammed barrels blew the breech apart and drove part of the hammer into the webbing of Hamilton's right hand. Both barrels were split wide open like a peeled banana. Slocum jerked his Colt and stuck it in Hamilton's side.

But Hamilton did not move. He stared at the jagged edge of the shotgun hammer as it stuck out of his palm. Slocum had thought there would have been much more damage.

"You're pretty lucky," Slocum said. "Now you jus' walk up the road to our camp. We need a little privacy."

The two men went up past the scrub juniper and down into the flat.

"Unbuckle your gun belt," Slocum said. "Let it drop. Now walk away. Stop. Sit on that rock an' pull out that busted hammer. You're makin' me nervous the way you keep lookin' at it."

Hamilton worked at it, wiggling it back and forth, with low, suppressed moans. Slocum looked at him with disgust. He walked across, grabbed the jagged hammer and yanked it out in one fast, hard pull. The blood oozed freely.

"Rough out here all alone, ain't it?"

"Whaddya want, Slocum?" Hamilton clasped his bleeding hand in the other.

Slocum, in one sense, knew what he wanted. He wanted revenge. On the other hand, he realized that he didn't know how he wanted it. He had waited months for this moment. He did not want the end to take a long time. He took no pleasure in torture.

Slocum wanted Hamilton dead. But he did not want to shoot him in cold blood. It had been different with Byron and Hogan. They would have shot him in the back without a second's hesitation. Slocum was not sure whether Hamilton would have done the same thing. It had the effect of holding him back.

"Where were you gonna meet your wife?"

Hamilton just stared at him.

"You—you gonna kill me an' go fer her?"

"I don't give a goddamn for your woman, Hamilton. She was pretty fine for an afternoon in a heavy rain—did she get all them hairpins together?"

Hamilton forgot he had dropped his gun belt. His hand flashed down and clawed at the empty air.

"Calm down," Slocum said. "She'll find some other damn fool easy enough. I jus' been wonderin' what your last few nights was like."

Dirty, Slocum knew. But he remembered Hamilton pulling hard at Bond's ankles to make him strangle.

Suddenly Slocum saw what a stranger to the country might think was the flash of a crow's wing sliding between two rocks on the opposite slope, above where the two bodies lay.

It was an Apache's head, angling down towards the two dead men. Then two more; then a pause; then one more.

They were after the Pinkertons' weapons. If he and Hamilton hadn't been attacked, Slocum knew it meant one thing: The Apaches only carried bows and arrows.

"I'm gonna leave you afoot, Hamilton," he said. "But I ain't gonna leave you without a gun. You jus' help yourself to Byron's. You pick it up an' don't look back. You jus' keep goin'. You turn around jus' once an' you'll be sorry. 'Cause I'm gonna keep you in my sights till you get far away. You hear?"

Hamilton nodded. He scrambled down the slope. At his appearance in the road the cautious movements on the slope opposite came to an abrupt halt. Slocum lay down with his Winchester ready.

He watched Hamilton cross the road and start upward, stumbling and cursing as he angled in and out of the rocks and boulders towards Byron's body.

The next step, as Slocum knew, was inevitable. The

Apaches could not afford to let him get the guns they coveted.

It came. Even at that distance he heard the *thump! thump!* of the bowstrings, and the thuds as the arrows hit home.

37

Slocum lifted his Winchester. In quick succession he fired four shots at the boulders.

The little valley bellowed with the sounds of the explosions, interspersed with the heartrending squeals of the bullets and the *crack!* of their impacts. Little sprays of gray rock dust spurted from the boulder surfaces.

He crawled quickly to another vantage point. He saw a swift blur of black hair moving upward. He fired three more shots to help the Apache along. Then, reloading, he crawled quickly ten yards away.

He squeezed off four more shots. That would let the Apaches think they had three men with Winchesters to deal with. Slocum knew they would come to the decision that the odds were too high, particularly since they hadn't managed to pick up a single gun. They'd go off for greener pastures, preferably a lonely sheepherder.

Slocum saw a dirty white breechclout slide between two junipers near the crest of the ridge opposite. He fired two shots, deliberately missing. Bits of bark spattered the air above the silent figure. If he had killed one, the others would find that their honor required that he be followed as long as possible. And an Apache, as Slocum well knew, could run 80 miles a day on foot. Since he would be moving with heavily laden burros, Slocum wanted none of that.

He waited five minutes. Then he worked his way

down the slope in a huge semicircle. He quickly crossed the road at a crouch. He worked his way upward again, his Winchester ready, till he saw Hamilton lying face down. He was still breathing.

Slocum turned him over.

One arrow had carried away the bridge of his nose and his left eye. The socket was full of coagulating blood. Another arrow had lodged in his throat.

When Slocum bent down, Hamilton tried to speak, but all he did was to blow a bloody froth on Slocum's face. Then he died.

The shadows of several soaring vultures passed over. Slocum stripped the clothes from the three dead men. He collected all their clothes and boots, all their guns and gun belts. There would be no way of identifying them.

There were more vultures now riding the updrafts, soaring and banking and waiting patiently. Slocum bunched everything under one arm and carried it down to the road. No one would ever know who they were. If they were ever found.

He threw a saddle blanket over Byron's horse.

There would be towns ahead of him like beads on a string. And women, too, like beads on another string. He looked at his hand. It was still bleeding. And a few more scars this time around. He cinched the saddle tight.

He wondered how long the money would last. It had never lasted long before.

Down on the lower river the Mexicans fired three shots across the river when anyone died: for the Father, the Son and the Holy Ghost.

Slocum wondered if anyone would ever do that for him when his time came. It would be nice to be remembered.